DIEGO

An MC Romance (Outlaw Souls Book 5)

HOPE STONE

GET FREE BOOKS!

Join Hope's newsletter to stay updated with new releases, get access to exclusive bonus content and much more!

Join Hope's newsletter here.

Tap here to see all of Hope's books.

Join Hope's Readers Group on Facebook.

DIEGO

Riding on the wings of freedom. Or as close as a man can come to it. I weaved slowly through the Pacific Highway traffic, the wind breezing past my face and the soft throttle of my Harley-Davidson leading me to my next destination. My chopper took me where I needed to be. Right now the road was leading to an unknown destination somewhere along the Californian coast. Just how I liked it. Things had changed drastically since Ryder took over from Padre as president of the Outlaw Souls. The chapter roster was switching up and people were being shuffled around the chessboard. I wanted out. My restless bones wanted someplace fresh and new. Someplace where people didn't know my name. With the changeover, my nomad patch stripes came into full effect and I got my chance.

"It's what Padre would have wanted. The floor is yours." Yoda, Padre's brother and chapter chaplain, sealed it at the Blue Dog Saloon meeting before I left. Music to my ears because the town of La Playa was...well, played out.

"You've officially been given your nomad stripes. Padre

always wanted to open a new chapter and expand the operation," Yoda explained.

"Then I'm the man to do it."

"Job's all yours, Diego. I approve of it." Yoda nodded while shaking my hand.

My essentials were neatly packed in my leased apartment. Ready to go. I would sort out the rest from wherever I landed. My heart had been calling me to leave for years. But I'd met someone that slowed my progress down. A beautiful woman. After things went sour with Crystal, I felt a sense of relief. I still wanted to remain loyal to the chapter, but the desperate ache to spread my wings made me jump at the chance to leave.

My chopper continued gliding smoothly through the California traffic as my stomach rumbled, telling me it was about time to stop and eat. No sad goodbyes and no heavy hearts either. I wasn't the man for that. When I moved on I liked to cut it clean. I planned on staying within the borders of California. I would know when to put the kickstand down. My plan was to check in somewhere and land where I felt best. That was as far as I got with it.

Thinking back to when I first met, things with Crystal had probably deteriorated over time. I used to frequent Marty's every Friday night. One Friday, I rode in solo and parked myself in a good spot. A mixed crowd of both men and women were out for the night, crimson lighting flooding the stage. I'd found myself a nice little spot close by. I was ready to kick back with some entertainment, maybe drop a little change. A tanned blonde with legs for days, ample curves and a pouty mouth graced the stage, making me sit up. Her moves on the stripper pole were more sensual than the other girls, not so grimy. The difference with her was her body looked natural and soft—no enhancements like I saw with the other strippers.

"Who the hell is that?" I'd tapped the shoulder of the bartender Alice, who I was on a first-name basis with. She put my beer in front of me.

"Ah, you like the look of her? That's Crystal, she just started here last week." I inched forward to get a better look. Her eyes met mine and I knew it was on. That was all it took with me. Eye contact. Took a few more visits before anything ramped up between us.

One midnight hour two years ago, that changed as Crystal slid towards me. "You come here all the time. I think it's about time you take me on a date." A long tongue suggestion and a kitten crawl across the stage would get you a date real quick with me.

"Sure. We can work something out." Heavy breasts jiggled as she swayed like fluid water to her feet.

"Sounds good, big boy. Meet you after my set. Drop them fifties right in here." She pointed to the elastic of her g-string. Of course I did. Any man in their right mind would. Just like that, we got started in a relationship that lasted two years. I grew to love her. But it wasn't enough. We got into it one night at my place.

"I don't want to strip anymore. I have enough saved to take a break for a while. Can't we think about taking the next step? I want a family with you." That cutesy voice I liked had become whiny to me, making my skin crawl as soon as she said it.

"It's not what I want. I'm not ready to settle down right now. I respect that's what you want. But honey, it's not for me." The tears flowed, and I comforted her as best I could. I knew the man I was inside.

"I didn't mean it. I mean, I can live without them. I just thought we had something." Crystal stroked my face and I left her with a kiss.

"We did, but it's run its course. If you want kids, I don't

want to rob you of that decision." I rubbed her hands. I wanted to have some level of compassion. "You're going to find someone just your vibe. I'm not your guy." Sometimes my honesty got me into trouble. Led to heartbreak. Might be part of the reason my name Diego the "Dog" Christopher fit me. Women never called me that to my face, thankfully. My devilish charm usually won them over. I remained friends with most of the women I banged. Even had a few of them on replay. Just depended on the season and the timing. But I treated all of them with the respect they deserved, which was why they kept coming back. Others in the club might have argued I got my nickname because of my loyalty.

So that was how it was left. No ties. Just the wind puffing up the back of my jacket and a hamburger joint coming up. I'd been riding for three hours and that was about my limit in any given stretch. Time to let my long limbs have a rest. Standing six feet two could have its advantages, but on a bike, it could tighten up the legs a little. I kinda wished I'd taken the coastal route. To have some of the ocean spray hit me in the face along the way. But for some reason, I'd chosen to stick to the Pacific Highway. The sign said "Bakersfield" as I pulled up to an old-school diner. I parked and stretched, taking in the clear blue California sky. A few large trucks were parked on the gravel driveway as I pushed through the screen door. The familiar sizzle of hamburgers on the grill and the distinct smell of onions made my mouth water. *Wouldn't mind a beer as well.* However, I was riding so I'd wait. A Mom and Pop hamburger joint, right up my alley. Anytime I rode out and found a good place to stop off for food, I stored it in the memory bank for the next ride. A few truckers were in the booths, making their stops and reading the paper. The sound of the radio flowed through the diner.

"Hey, good looking. On a stop? What can I get ya'?"

I gave the lady behind the counter a big grin. I liked her

spunk. A little dumpy probably, in her early fifties with brown hair stuck to her forehead from the Cali heat. She was wearing an old apron. It was just her out front with a rectangular peephole where the meals were being placed behind the counter. An older man with a net was whipping up the meals in the back. I looked up at the chalk menu board.

"Yep. Just passing through. I'm looking at that mega burger. I'll take it. Don't leave anything out," I replied.

"Okay." She laughed and her stomach heaved along with her. "That's a mighty fine bike you got out there." She pointed to it.

"Sure is. My pride and joy."

"I can see why. We get some bikers that roll through here from time to time. Check out those mags in the rack if you want." She pointed to a pile of magazines in the middle of the diner. "Take a seat and I'll bring your burger out. Help yourself to water on the side there."

"Will do." My meal came out ten minutes later. I devoured the juicy hamburger with everything included and washed it down with juice. I sat out front of the takeaway, flicking through a local bike magazine. I stopped a few pages in. A bunch of old dudes in riding gear, getting together for rides. But where? Merced. I looked again. *So they like their bikes up there.* The article mentioned they tried to get a club going with no success. Disbanded. As good a place as any to start. Might take some legwork to get it going, but my instincts told me yes... *Merced, California, here I come.* The open road had become a sanctuary for me long ago. A place to unwind, to contemplate, to be free. Heading to Merced was no exception. I could lay down roots and set up shop for a while. *Yep. Might be nice, see how I like it.*

I'd been married once to Catarina. Fresh out of high school and struggling to make ends meet. "You're too young to get married, Diego. Why don't you wait?" my sweet mother warned me, but we were blinded. I was nineteen at the time and I wanted what I wanted.

"Stay out of it. I love Catarina and she loves me. We're getting married." Five good years or so, I'd thought. Put my heart and soul into it as a man. We thought we would never want to be apart from one another. *Fairy tales don't last forever; sometimes they end badly.* A vivid flashback came to mind as I sat in Bakersfield.

"What the hell is going on? Get the fuck out of my house!" Some weedy dude was bumping and grinding with my wife. "Is this why you've been working late?" I screamed. I nearly lost my mind when I caught her.

"You were never home and I was lonely." Catarina's sad eyes filled with tears, staring back at me. The irony was that I was working hard as a mechanic at my local garage trying to make ends meet. Catarina worked as a secretary in a doctor's office. The divorce sucked the life right out of me. Then add the drain on my little bank account and you could say I received the ultimate uppercut. After that, I vowed never to be committed again.

"I heard you're looking for members? I'm in, if you'll have me." That was the moment I joined the Outlaw Souls. Six years ago to the day and I never looked back. A brotherhood that would never abandon me, so I couldn't abandon them. I would support my fellow riders to the death.

Belly full and with a new resolve, I briefly looked over Merced on my phone. It was close to college campuses and the nearby Yosemite park. Good places to take day rides to.

I rode into Merced, California on a candy-coated sunset two and a half hours later to start my new life and a new chapter.

MISTY

The size of a clenched fist. The one muscle that does all the work. The illustrious aorta and master of the pulmonary valve function. The door to the lower heart chamber, allowing the pulmonary artery to do its work, pumping blood through the body.

My vision was blurring because of all the back and forth over the textbook pages. I was tired from trying to absorb information and retain it for my upcoming test. I was getting back to basics first and revisiting my knowledge of myocardial infarctions. In layman's terms, the heart attack. I was knee-deep in the study zone with anatomy books spread open to various pages at my study desk in my room. The sun streamed through my curtains, making it a little more bearable. My mug of strong coffee helped that along as well.

Funny that scientists say the heart holds more intelligence than the brain. It's the epicenter of the body. If my heart had such intelligence, why was I always getting stabbed in it? It made me think of Carlos. I raised my head up from my books, giving myself an eye break, and sipped on my coffee. The guy was a heartbreaker and dream killer – that was what I called him. The suave Mexican with jet-black hair, chiseled face, and well-toned physique. He was older than me by three years. I didn't know any better when he wormed his way into my life.

"Hey, pretty lady. You're waiting on your brother, right?" That silky voice entered my ears while I waited on Palo outside the clubhouse to give me a ride to my friend's house. When I looked at him, I thought he was mesmerizing. I thought he was a god. *My first mistake.*

We dated from the tender age of twenty-three on the low for three long years. He was part of the fucked-up motorcycle club – Las Balas. I shook my head at my stupidity as I listened to the birds chirp. As the hands of fate would have it, he left later down the track after we broke up. From that point on, I wanted nothing to do with Las Balas. Hard to deal with because my brother was involved with them, heavy.

"El Diablo's gone now. I can run the club the right way now." My older brother Palo had his sights set on being the next head of the club. He'd been riding with Las Balas a long time.

"I don't want nothing to do with the club. All that criminal activity is what Carlos was involved in. I'm studying to be a doctor and you need to keep that shit out of the house." My limits had been reached. The destruction and bloodshed that Las Balas caused was common knowledge to those in the know. I used to live with Carlos and got caught up in the lifestyle he provided. The cars, the shopping, the dinners and the sex. All that money could buy. Except that it couldn't make him keep his dick in his pants. I didn't know the extent of the cheating until we broke up.

It was exposed one night when I was out with my study partners from campus. Another Spanish chica approached me at a local bar.

"Ola. I see what he likes." Her long dark hair swung as she walked. She had olive skin and wore a skintight dress. I was halfway wasted at the time so I was paying little attention to her.

"What?" I slurred back at her.

"You Carlos's girl?" The bar was cranking and I was ready to get back out on the dance floor with my girls and this payasa was scanning me. Up and down. Up and down.

"Used to be. Not anymore." I could barely focus. I was that drunk. I was hanging on to the bar for support, laughing like a hyena. All I knew at that point was having fun. A damn good time in fact.

"I had him." She wiggled her manicured hand in my face. Then I watched as she turned and sashayed away. That happened a lot during the relationship, not just after the fact. But every time, Carlos sweet-talked me back off the ledge.

"Baby, she's lying. You can't believe nothing these chicas say." The pleading, the begging, and the puppy dog eyes. I somehow managed to take him back every time.

"No, it wasn't like that! I gave her a kiss on the cheek." He would always hunch his shoulders up like I was attacking him when I accused him. "You didn't see what you thought you saw." Toxic screaming matches followed pretty quickly after that. Some involved me throwing plates at his head. Blame it on my hot Spanish blood.

"*Estúpido!*" So the cycle continued where I cried and Carlos would wine and dine me right out of my clothes. Things would go back to being good for a few months. Like nothing happened.

"When you finish med school, you and I can get married. We can have a family." The guy was a compulsive liar and fed lies like cotton candy to every woman he met.

Then I would inevitably hear through the grapevine that he was together with other girls. The last straw was when I caught him red-handed. I walked into the bedroom. I had to adjust my eyes at first. It was as if they didn't want to absorb what they were witnessing. A slender girl riding on top of him, moaning in the middle of the act. In *our* bedroom. My heart fell apart right then and there. Our sheets soiled by this heifer. Cheated on more times than I could remember.

I let out a deep sigh at the memory. Carlos, with his swarthy looks, was one that my brother actually approved of. And he didn't approve of many. So I left. Packed right in the middle of the night.

"Don't leave! We can work this out! It's not a big deal, my heart is with you."

The texts and phone calls came for weeks, trying to win me back. And that was how I ended up living at the other end of my brother's house. My brother got on my nerves sometimes so I thought it best to get my own place in due course.

"I feel responsible," Palo said when I wept in his arms. "You should come live with me for a while 'till you get back on your feet."

I wasn't going to live with my parents. I wanted peace and quiet to study. They were never quiet over there. After that, let's just say the next time I saw Carlos out he had a black eye. My brother Palo had fixed him up and told him to stop calling me. For the most part, he was protective over me.

"I want you to finish medical school. That's what you wanted to do. Follow your dreams," he told me.

That was why my room consisted mostly of medical books. Wall to wall in fact. Among some other crowd favorites when I had time to read them. Attending the University of California's medical school left me very few hours for hobbies. But when I had time to party, it was on. I'd watched three of my loved ones pass on because of heart complications – misdiagnosed.

In a lot of ways, my aspiration to be a heart surgeon stemmed from this. I wanted to be the one giving the right diagnosis. To walk in and tell the family, "He's going to pull through. He made it."

Not the dreaded doom and gloom like when my uncle passed away. I would never forget that day. The doctor had pulled down his teal mask with a grim face. "Unfortunately, your uncle didn't make it. We did our best." *No.* I didn't want to hear that anymore. I wanted to save lives. To help people. My family members weren't helping themselves, though. They ate all sorts of heavy, rich Puerto Rican foods. Part of my culture, no running from that with all our large family gatherings.

I happened to be the pioneering one in my family. The first one to go to college, a foreign concept to my extended family. They didn't understand why I couldn't be at every family gathering and doing things with them at every turn. I was looking forward to letting loose with my friends.

DIEGO

Not bad at all. Merced. As soon as I let the engine stop and felt the ground underneath my feet, I knew I was in the right place. Slight breeze and mild California weather so far. A mighty fine place to start a chapter. I checked into the Studio 6 motel, as good a place as any to hang up my biker boots for the night. Nothing fancy about it, just a comfortable bed and a nightcap. That was all a man like me needed. A pretty young teenager behind the reception greeted me.

"Hi. How can I help you?"

I greeted her back with a smile.

"I want to check in for three nights."

"Let me see here. Looks like we have a room available; number 36B. Do you want the continental breakfast as well?" she asked.

"Sounds good." I winked at her, taking the keys off her hands.

It was a plain room, all the amenities I required. Fresh towels, a TV, the little packet soaps, and a desk with two chairs. It would be okay for the short term, my plan being to find permanent accommodation and get set up. I shot off a text to Ryder.

Made it. Merced is the place. Checking in.

I didn't expect a call back right away. I just wanted to let him know out of respect. Ryder's schedule would have increased right along with his responsibilities. Now, he was the president with big shoes to fill. Padre's death hit me hard. Another reason for the move. Too many places around La Playa reminded me of him. I recalled one time at Blue Dog Saloon at midnight over whiskey sours.

"You know, Diego. I started this chapter with a dream in mind. We've defended our turf. We've even fought wars with other bike gangs to hold our place. Outlaw Souls will always live on. The stories I could tell you...man. The life I've known would blow you away." From Padre's leathery skin, his street knowledge and timelines etched around his eyes, I knew he was telling the truth. He'd lived a hard and fast life. I learned so much from him. One conversation was forever etched in my brain.

"Loyalty is everything. If people are loyal to you, you never have to worry. The trouble is how to gain and keep that loyalty. Now that's where the magic formula is." He would let his cigar hang out of his mouth without lighting it. "There's honor in that." A brilliant mind taken to the other side. I looked in the hotel mirror after I checked in. I pulled at my beard a little. Not a full one, just enough to call it that. I could do with a shape-up. And to hit the gym. I carried myself well normally. I just noticed the edges blurring a little. Some softness. Nothing a month or two in the gym wouldn't sort out. But one step at a time. Tomorrow would be the day to scout these places out. I decided against heading to the hotel restaurant; plenty of time for that. I wanted to get a feel for the real Merced. I was a diner man, so that was where I headed to.

I rode out a little, not too far from where I was staying. I eased the bike into the Black Bear Diner. A red brick building set up like a modern-day diner. Made sense they'd call it that. Merced wasn't far from the home of the black bears. I made a mental note to make Yosemite Park the first official ride for the motorcycle chapter. The freshness of the air up here made me appreciate my new surroundings. Pine trees, raging rivers, closer to the wilderness of California. I breathed in the crisp air and entered the diner. The place had a nice beat to it. Humble. Again, nothing fancy. A few people talking in corner booths, but nothing out of the ordinary. I had a hankering for another burger and fries with a whole lotta ketchup, and a window seat. A strawberry shake to wash it down with would put me in the right mood for anything. I made a mental note to hit the gym or hike next week. My fast metabolism would burn it right off. I was lucky like that.

I sat down near the window to look out. I picked up the local paper to get a feel for some things in town. I checked in on the menu, hoping they had what I wanted. Yes, I was in luck. My mouth started to water, imagining the taste of the burger. A young waitress approached. At first, she didn't look up from her notepad.

"Hi, sir. Welcome to the Black Bear Diner. What can I get for you today?"

"Hi. I will have the big bear burger with extra ranch sauce, a strawberry shake and fries with ketchup." I'd been told by many – mostly women – that I had a seductive voice. Might have been my Argentine accent that reared its head from time to time. Especially if I had a drink or I was angry. One that made women pay attention. Her eyes shot up and I watched her reaction. She was a cutie—too young, though. From her youthful appearance, I would say nineteen or twenty. Her face broke into a wide smile.

"Uh- okay. Would you like anything else?" She stared a little too long. I let her look.

"No. I'm good. But here's something for you." I gave her a tip. *Sweet kid.*

"Thank you so much," she gushed as her cheeks flushed with pink. The smile got a little bit wider as she scampered back behind the counter. Being the good citizen I was, I didn't want her being too bored at work. She'd probably been serving customers all day.

I had a nice vantage point from my booth so I saw her before she spotted me. A real Spanish beauty, had to be or at least she had some Spanish blood in her. I hoped it would be me soon. Long auburn hair, dimples and the eyes of a seductress. Her voluptuous body was poured into red jeans with a black tight-fitting top and a jean jacket. From head to toe, she did it for me. Made me do a double-take just like the waitress did when she saw me. She was a bad mama jama. Three other women were with her. But she held her own in the group. I sized her up. Nice height, fit right in the size of my palm. She wouldn't have been taller than five feet six. Petite in size, feminine, and my heart started pumping just that little bit harder. A nice welcome to Merced. She looked like she was laughing and sharing a joke with her friends; she hadn't turned her head my way yet.

The door swung open and the waitress made her way to me with my order. I smelled it coming. My stomach growled on cue.

One of the girls from the group said, "Wow, that looks so good. I'm going to get what he's having." I guessed when they saw who the burger was being delivered to, their tune changed.

"Forget the burger. I will take the guy who ordered it." I turned my back to them, but they were loud enough to be within earshot of me. I smirked to myself. *Let the games begin.*

"I agree." Girlish talk and giggles. The Black Bear Diner was shaping up to be good for my ego. I decided to turn and flash them a grin, but when I looked back, the hot girl crew were ordering.

"Here you go. Big bear burger and fries with extra ranch and a strawberry shake." The waitress blocked my view and delivered my order to me.

"Thank you. This looks great." I concentrated on the burger and filling a need. I sank my teeth into it. It tasted as good as it looked. I sucked down the thickness of the strawberry shake too quick and gave myself an ice cream headache. Damn, it was good, though. Out of my peripheral, it looked like the girls had taken up residence along the other end of the long window bench I was at. I knew they were watching me. I heard the hushed tones. A few little giggles. Made me smile. I refocused for a minute and studied the paper I had. I wanted to see if there were any warehouse spaces available. Better yet, any old repair shops that I could step into without having to do too much legwork on them.

I was halfway through my burger and feeling satisfied. My number one pick from the hot girl crew was sashaying toward me. I gave her the once-over. She asked for it. Especially with the way she glided over to me. She was shaped like an hourglass, so much better up close. Feline olive-green eyes. I'd never seen them that color before. *Thank God for women.* A cute upturned nose and gorgeous plump lips. She looked like dessert to me.

"Excuse me?" She came across as demure as she spoke.

"Hi." I kept my response simple. I wanted to hear what she had to say.

"Umm. Is that your bike out there?" She pointed out the window to my chopper with flames on the side.

"Yeah. That's my bike. You ride?" A moment. A serious spark of desire circling between us both. Real serious. She gave me the same once-over I gave her. I admired her boldness to approach me. Generally, I was the one to hunt.

If you wanna see me, just say the word. I'd planned to approach her on the way out. I wanted to drop my number off to her. I had no shame about that type of thing. If I saw a woman I wanted, I let her know. The rest I left up to her. She licked her lips.

"I'm no stranger to bikes. Is it a Harley?" She was flirting. I liked the game. I decided I would play along.

"Uh-huh. It's a Harley. Maybe I can take you for a ride sometime." She pointed her thumb back to her girlfriends, who were laughing in the background.

"My girls didn't think I would come over and ask you."

I tapped the seat next to me for her to sit down. I eyed her well-defined legs as she crossed them in an elegant way.

"I don't know why. I'm a likable guy. I don't bite." *Much.* She flicked her hair behind her shoulder. She had this irresistible quality that made me want to get closer to her. "Diego."

"I knew it." She fluttered her long lashes at me. She had my full attention and I'd stopped eating. Not too many things made me do that. "You're Spanish, aren't you?"

"I'm from Argentina originally." I still could see her girlfriends having a side conversation about us, but my focus most definitely was on this beauty in front of me.

"I'm Puerto Rican. Nice to meet you. I'm Misty." I grabbed Misty's hand, the electricity transported from my hand to hers. I planted a kiss on it. She blushed. *Damn*, she was fine.

"Ola, mamacita. You look beautiful. You're here with your friends?"

"Thank you and sort of. I'm having a little study break." I assessed the situation. She looked to be mid-twenties from what I saw.

"Okay. What are you studying?"

"I'm in med school right now to be a doctor," she said proudly. A slow grin came over my face. "What?" She drew back from me with a smile. "Why'd you look like that?" she asked.

"Well. I don't mean to offend you and come off corny. But if you were my doctor I would definitely be claiming I was sick every day." I sucked down a little of my strawberry shake and basked in her aura.

"You're funny. Let's hope you don't get sick. I think you're pretty fine too, for what it's worth." She gave me a sexy smile as she said it.

"Thank you." My brain snatched me to another place. *Get settled and then worry about getting some ass.* "Well, I hope your food's not getting cold over there." I nodded in the direction of her friends.

"Uh yeah..." She seemed confused by my sudden coolness. "Nice to meet you."

"See you around then."

Her emerald eyes shone back at me, making me smile.

"I hope so." I got a kick out of watching her hips sway back and forth as she walked back to her friends. I gazed out the window for a minute. Did that just happen? I missed the moment because next time I looked up, I saw her friends waving at me as they left the diner. *Shit.* I could have gotten her number for later. She caught me off-guard, that was why. A glint of something captured my attention. I looked to the tiled floor. A bankcard. *Shit.* She'd left it behind. I picked it up and on instinct, like a bolt of lightning, I ran out to get it back to her. I missed again. In the parking lot I saw the navy blue sedan drive off. I put my hands behind my head. *Shit.* Two options were being presented, the way I saw it. Take it to the front counter and have them get it back to her. Surely she'd retrace her steps back to the diner? Or I could keep it and use it as an excuse to contact her. I chose the latter. I definitely wanted to see her again.

I rode back to the hotel, a semi-satisfied man. Before I turned in for the night, the image of Misty popped up. Smart and sexy. I had her credit card in my hands, looked to be a platinum black card. *Interesting.* M. Narvaez was the name on it. Most definitely a Puerto Rican surname. Couldn't be too many Mistys around. My first stop was to get more information; the internet. I typed in her full name. A few options popped up. A Facebook profile picture with hearts around it appeared with her face in it. Jackpot. I logged into my Facebook and requested her as a friend.

A couple of hours later as I lay in bed watching TV, my phone pinged. She'd accepted my request. I sent her a message.

"Hey, you left your black card at the diner. Let me know where you want me to drop it off. Nice to meet you. Diego."

Ten seconds later.

"OMG! You have it! Can we meet near McDonald's downtown in the next few hours?"

"Sure I can meet you. I have a request though."

"What is it?"

"Are you up for a coffee? I would love to spend some time with you."

Twenty seconds later she responded.

"I would love that. "

"In 20 mins ok?"

"Perfect see you then."

I showered and took the opportunity to shave up. Not bad for thirty-six. I held the strong jawline of my father. My ice-blue eyes came from my mother. Time to meet the Puerto Rican princess.

Merced in the evening had it going on. People were out

doing their thing. A few other guys on bikes, I noticed. Ducatis. Harleys. All of this bode well for me. I took it as another sign I was in the right place. I would take her home in a heartbeat, that was how fine she was. I would override that voice that told me I needed to focus on the chapter first. No questions asked. If she was down so was I. I picked up my second helmet which I always carried with me and put it in my carrier bag on the back of my bike. I pulled up to the McDonald's minutes later and waited. Cars moved in and out of the parking lot. it was only half full. The stars were out and shining bright. It was about nine o'clock. I watched as Misty stepped out of her Honda and made her way over to my bike.

"Hey. Thank you so much! I didn't even know it was missing. Imagine if someone got a hold of it," she gushed.

"It's all good. In safe hands with me. I only spent ten thousand. You'll be okay." I broke into a corny grin. She laughed and lightly tapped my forearm in response. I was still sitting on my bike and resting there. Her touch made me want to drag her into me and take over her lips.

"You're a funny guy, huh?" She tilted her head with interest.

"Sometimes." A moment went by, the still cool of the night making me think she might be getting cold. She was dressed the same as when I saw her earlier. The McDonald's light pole shone an amber light right on her pretty face.

"Soooo, do you want to get outta here and we can go grab a coffee?" I asked. She looked at me for a minute as if considering her options.

"I don't know. Can I trust you? I mean—I don't know you so well to be getting on the back of your bike." The subtle pick-up of the wind had her moving strands of loose hair from her face.

"Sure you know me. I'm the guy from the diner who

picked up your black card and returned it to you the same night," I ventured. Shyly, she crossed her legs over and breathed out loud.

"Okay, you got me... Fuck it!" She gestured with defeat. "Let's go. Get me to the coffee shop alive, okay?"

"You think I wanna get killed? I'm all about safety. Check back there, your helmet awaits." I gestured to the back of the bike. A light hand pressed on the top of my shoulder as she maneuvered to sit behind me and I put my helmet on.

"I can't believe you! How did you know I would want to get on the bike with you?" she exclaimed.

"Haha. I didn't." She didn't ask me any questions. She knew about bikes, I could tell. No fear at all. "Do you know the rules?" I spoke through my helmet, turning side-on.

"For sure. Lean when you lean...and hold on tight," she replied.

"Good lady. Let's do this." I flicked the plexiglass of my helmet cover down and waited for her to get situated. Her arms wrapped around me, her fingers splayed across my abdominals. My body responded with an increase of fire running through my veins. A few streets over, I pulled up. I saw an intimate coffee shop with dim lighting. We parked and entered. I opened the door for her like the gentleman I was raised to be. Soft jazz music played in the background with golden light enhancing the space. More like a lounge bar than a coffee shop. We found a spot near the front window that faced the street. We slid into the front and ordered our drinks.

"So are you from here?" she asked.

"No. I just moved here today."

"Oh really? Why Merced?" she quizzed. The waitress came to our table not long after with our coffees.

"Why not?" I replied. "Why medicine?"

"Why not?" she retorted with a smirk. Sassy and could keep up with me. She was starting to tick a lot of boxes for me. "There you go with that funny guy business again."

"You started it," I challenged.

"No, really, why did you move here?" She didn't let up about it. She possessed that fire in her eyes. I wonder if she had that same fiery energy in the bedroom. My dick was dying to find out.

"I wanted a fresh start to spread my wings. Plus, I think it's a good place to ride." As soon as I mentioned riding, her demeanor changed drastically. "What, you don't like bikes? You seem to know your way around one," I responded.

"I do for sure. I know a few people who ride." Her eyes grew distant as she said it.

"Okay, that's a good thing. Nothing like being on the back of a bike," I said. Her hands were tapping the side of her cup and she appeared to be agitated by my comments. I switched it up.

"Do you have a special field you want to work in as a doctor?" Her eyes went dreamy and the mood shifted right side up.

"I want to be a cardiologist. To work on people's hearts."

"Admirable. I like it."

"Just means I'm going to be in school for a *loooong* time." She rolled her eyes.

"It sounds like it'll be worth it in the end." What didn't she have going for her? But right now I had a firm no-strings policy. This one looked like she had some strings in her bag.

"For sure it will." We skipped around the way of things, keeping the conversation light. My conscience was telling me not to take her back to my hotel room. The lady was trying to become a doctor, after all. I knew I would see her again. That was a given.

After some silence and staring out the window, I said to her, "Okay, little lady. Are you ready to go?" Misty rubbed her hands over her thighs. She was shivering a little even though she had a jacket on. I shook off my jacket and put it around her shoulders. Just me and my T-shirt left. Truthfully, I didn't feel the cold that much.

"Here. Stay warm 'til I get you back to your car." I gazed into those cat green eyes. She beamed in appreciation.

"Thank you, you're a gentleman."

I paid at the counter and we headed out the door. I handed her the helmet I had for her. "One more time for the road." Her sensual lips curved into a cute smile. Merced was a place this man could definitely get used to. The navy blue sky was lit up with stars for us as I enjoyed the freshness of the night air hitting my face. The parking lot lights were out when we got back. I let the engine die down and Misty got off.

"Thank you so much for tonight. I had a great time. You're sweet." If she only knew the wolf inside of me wanted to drag her back to my hotel bed. I let her run with it. She unzipped my jacket and gave it back to me.

"You're welcome." Goosebumps were raised on her arms. I could see them in the moonlight. I didn't want to hold her up. "I won't beat around the bush. I want to see you again." She held my gaze in the moonlight.

"Let's see," she purred. The sexual tension was right here, hanging in the air. I didn't move an inch. She stepped to the bike and I reeled her in with one arm. My lips sought out hers and made a deadly assault, opening the vault. She returned the intensity and our tongues explored. Her breasts pressed against me, making me want to lay her down on the bike. Before it got too heavy, I released her.

"How's that for seeing?" I said huskily. She lingered, fingering my jacket.

"That works," she replied, breathless. "You know how to find me, Diego."

"No doubt." Her sexy tight ass walked to her car, leaving me enthralled. *Right on, Merced.*

MISTY

The next few days after meeting with the hottie Diego floated by. My feet felt like they didn't touch the ground. I was in such a euphoric place. My classes were not a problem, and any annoying lecturers weren't an issue either.

Diego had shoulder-length dirty blond hair tied back. All tousled and wild like him. Rugged manly features and a face kissed by the sun. He had a three o'clock shadow, not five o'clock. His toned, thick muscular thighs and well-defined arms would wrap around me soon enough. I planned on it happening. Ever since I saw him sitting on his lonesome in the Black Bear diner. My study friends were salivating over him, but I was the one to approach. When I saw those piercing ocean-blue eyes, that cemented it for me. I had to go talk to him.

We had a date coming up, a day trip to Yosemite. I decided Diego was worth taking the day off for. My panties were wet just thinking about him. One thing was bothering me and it included my knucklehead brother.

"Hey, sis. What you got going on today?"

I grabbed my piece of toast as it popped up from the

toaster. "I've got class. How about you?" I probed. His eyes were cagey, moving around like darts. He didn't answer straight away. "*Palo*," I asked again, expecting an answer.

"I gotta take care of some business, you know, then I'm heading into work," Palo relayed softly.

I narrowed my eyes at him. "What kind of business do you need to take care of?"

Palo rubbed his shaved head back and forth, avoiding my gaze. "Business... Do you really wanna know?" he responded with his slight Spanish accent. I put my hand on my hip and blocked him from leaving the kitchen. The rage was building inside of me. My brother wasn't that tall. He stood a few inches over me. But nothing that would make me scared of him.

"Yeah. I do. That's why I asked you." I glared at him.

"Look. I'm in the lead for the presidency. The vote is tonight," he said with a guilty expression. Shockwaves ran through my system.

"What the fuck do you mean, presidency, mano? El Diablo just got murdered!" Palo had the same greenish eyes as me, except with more hazel accents. He tried to soothe me by grabbing my arm.

"Hey. I want to change things. The other guys listen to me. I can make it better. That's part of my familia too. Just like you are." My eyes welled up with angry tears. I didn't want the same fate for my brother as El Diablo.

"You're stupid! You'll get killed! What have they ever done for you that's so great, huh?" I pressed.

"Don't start this mess again, Misty. You're taken care of, aren't you? I'm paying your way through medical school. Without the club, you wouldn't have been able to get there," he responded with passion. A wave of emotional guilt washed over me.

"Don't you dare!" My Spanish fire raged in my blood,

ready to burn him. "I would have bagged groceries if I had to so you didn't have to be part of Las Balas. I never wanted your dirty money to cover me. You fool!" I spat back. His jaw clenched and he gritted his teeth. I didn't care. My brother wouldn't harm a hair on my head.

"I'm going to do what I want, when I want, and that's just it. Hypocritical of you since you accepted the gifts from Carlos!" He came back at me. A low blow. The glare of try-me was written all over his face. I let it drop. Every time we got into an argument, it was about Las Balas. I had to focus all my energy on my studies, so I refused to go back and forth with him for too long.

"My thing is that...I'm scared because now I feel you'll be a target. I didn't know what Carlos was doing. But I didn't ask either." I softened. "Why can't you understand that? Why now?" My spirit was vexed. Behind Palo was this sense of urgency that irked me. We were pretty close, but this time, hidden secrets were in the mix. I ate my toast and drank down my juice quickly. I didn't want to be late for class. Palo kept rubbing his head.

"I'm sorry. That was wrong for me to say," he sighed. "This club is a community though. We stand together; a few rotten eggs don't mean we fall apart. I'm going to end up president. It's happening." His eyes were like a tiger's. When he spoke, people listened. Ladies loved him as well. I waited, wanting to hear him out. "I'll fix it. Make it right. I'm not about violence in the club. But sometimes you have to do what you have to do." As soon as the animated version of my brother emerged, I got ready for a major speech. I crossed my arms, anticipating it. "El Diablo had to go. He put a black cloud over the whole club." His arm reached out to span in a circle. "Now. Me." He beat his chest with his fist. "I will be the man to restore us. All of my brothers will stand with me. Legit business dealings. Family rides. Helping the community.

When we stand together, we can achieve much. We can move mountains. But divided, we fall."

I paused. All of his points were valid. I let him continue:

"If we crumble now, the street hustlers win. We must crusade for the right causes, Misty. Just like you want to save lives, so do I." That hit hard. I had no rebuttal.

"Two sides of the coin, aren't we? Passionate about family," I responded softly. His tight face softened, and he pulled me in for a hug.

"I love you, little one. I get it you're worried. It's going to be fine though. I swear."

"Promise?"

He held out his pinky finger and tugged at mine. "Pinky swear."

I smiled. "I can't stop you, but know I'm not happy about it," I grumbled. He chuckled and grabbed my cheek.

"I know. See you when I'm looking at you." He winked and left me standing in the kitchen. I sighed and looked to the heavens, asking God to protect my brother.

I made it to anatomy class right on time. My study partner and African American friend Shauna squeezed in beside me. We were in the lab today, looking at anatomical models.

"Hey, girl! How are you? Did you end up getting your card back from Mr. Hottie?"

I fanned myself in response. She laughed.

"Yes, I sure did. And hottie is right!" We clasped hands together. We had about twenty people in our class and we were set to look directly at dead bodies and examine them. The life and times of a medical student.

"I hope the smell of formaldehyde doesn't make me barf." She held on to my arm dramatically.

"How the hell are you going to be a doctor if you can't handle bad smells?" I threw back at her.

"Umm. Good point." She wagged her finger at me. "Yep, I concur. Might be time for me to reassess." Other students from our class rolled in and Mrs. Sinclair spoke.

"Hello, all my bright and beautiful med students. Today we're going to go straight to matters of the heart. We are going to take a look at some healthy hearts and some not-so-healthy hearts."

Shauna wrinkled her nose in disgust. I tapped her lightly. Mrs. Sinclair, a lady in her late fifties and the former head of a surgical ward, was someone I had respect for. I really wanted to pay attention to this class. She'd worked at one of the most renowned hospitals in the country.

"Put your gloves on at the front of the class and we'll wheel them out one by one. I want you to dig deep today and tell me what's wrong with each of them. Time to put all that theory into action," she said.

I concentrated hard and was able to pick up most of the defects with each case and scenario presented. I missed a couple of things, but that was about it.

After class, I scrubbed the essence of dead hearts from my body. Sometimes it took a while to shake off the stench. Students poured out of the class one by one. Shauna and I stepped out and onto campus grounds.

"Hey!" Shauna grabbed my elbow. She had a lot of spunk and loved to party when she could, like me. "Why don't we go to The Partition on Friday night? Get Rob, Celine and Michael to come with us?" she asked eagerly. I had my date on Saturday with Diego, so plenty of time to sleep in on Saturday and recover.

"Hell yeah! Let's do it. They have the best cocktails there too."

"I got class with Celine and Rob today and I'll let them in on it." Shauna beamed.

"Sounds like a plan to me for sure."

DIEGO

The rest of my day ran smoothly on campus. I felt like I was getting somewhere with my studies. That at least I had a solid enough knowledge for when my hospital rounds began. Tomorrow was Friday and I had a lot of studying to do before I could even think about the outfit I wanted to shake my money-maker in on Friday. When I left for the day, I resumed my studies in my room. The house was quiet. Palo must have been out. I was so hard at the books that I didn't realize it was eight o'clock and I hadn't eaten anything. I stretched and made my way to the kitchen to whip up some eggs. My phone pinged. Diego.

"Hey beautiful. Checking in. See you at 10 this Saturday?"
"Looking forward to it. Heart emoji."
"Wear your hiking boots!"
"Stilettos work?" I giggled out loud.
"That's for later in the night... devil emoji."

My heart started to beat fast. I'd never seen anything like him. Pure power, I could feel it in him. Every fiber of my Latino being wanted to be taken over by him. The man was yummy. I made something to eat, grabbed a coffee, and resumed the books until midnight.

California brought on the sunshine and good vibes the next day. I had a bounce in my step and I knew Diego had a lot to do with that. Friday, as far as college was concerned, was my favorite day. A half-day. If I worked hard, my motto was to play hard. I'd seen and talked to my friends who'd made it through their residency and worked in the emergency room.

"Girl, we are on call twenty-four-seven. Make the most of your college days now."

After arriving home from the day, I pulled out all my potential outfits that I wanted to wear. I FaceTimed Shauna.

"Hey, girl, what are you wearing? How about this one?" I asked as I put the phone on my dresser drawers. She put her nose close to the phone. I could see up her nostrils. She stepped back.

"Girl. No. I can see your va-jay-jay. Try again." I stifled a laugh.

"You're no fun. Okay, wait! Lemme see." I held up a classy black dress with the shoulders cut out. She gave me a thumbs-up.

"There you go! That's the one." She approved. I danced around a little.

"Okay. I will see you in half an hour, I'm calling the Uber for then," I explained. Shauna nodded on the screen.

"Okay, girl. Celine and Rob will be with me. The rest of the crew are going to meet us there a little later. I got a banging outfit, you'll see it when you get here."

"Whoo-hoo! I'm so excited. I can't wait."

"Me neither. I've been waiting for cocktail hour all week," she sighed. I clicked off and put the phone down. I loved to party. Part of my bloodline's culture. My whole family would party all the time. Every celebration you could think of, we would be dancing, drinking and embracing life.

My brother sauntered in about the same time as I was heading out the door.

"Esta bella, sis," he said, looking me over. He gave me the thumbs-up. I kissed him on the cheek.

"Thank you. I gotta go." I headed for the front door.

"Where you going?" he inquired.

"The Partition."

"Ah, a couple of the boys are headed there later on I think. I'm not sure."

"Are you sending them to spy on me?" I asked as I pushed past his left shoulder.

DIEGO

Palo frowned at me. "Nope. I just know they mentioned it."

"Who?" I enquired.

"I never got to know them. They joined the chapter not so long ago." Palo stopped short of saying anything else.

"What?" I probed.

"Nothing, except have a good time and call me if you need anything." He kissed my cheek and hurried down the other end of the house. I caught the Uber to Shauna's place and knocked on the door.

"Ayyy." She grabbed both my shoulders and looked at my dress. "Now that's a killer dress! You are smoking, mama. I'm loving that lipstick. We ready to rip it up or what?" I grinned back at her. She was wearing a bright yellow dress with strappy silver heels. Shauna loved her flamboyant colors.

"You know it!" I clicked my fingers with attitude and walked in. Celine came around the corner from the living room.

"You look amazing! I haven't seen you in forever." She beamed. Celine was a cute redhead with pale Irish skin, studying to be a nurse at the University of California. She had on an emerald dress that suited her creamy skin along with red lipstick.

"So do you, look at you!" She did a little spin and Rob stepped to the front as well.

"Hey, Rob, you look handsome." He did. Rob was in his first year already of his residency and kept us in the loop of what to expect. It was rare to catch him. He was tall with dark hair, blue eyes and pale skin that made him stand out.

"Why, thank you. You look sexy. On the prowl tonight?" His eyes danced with mischief and his lips threatened to curl into a smile.

"I mean, maybe. Depends," I replied saucily with a wiggle of my hips. Truth was I wasn't. My interest was firmly focused on Diego. I gave Shauna a high-five and we all burst into spontaneous fits of laughter.

"Please don't ever change." Rob shook his head and bent to kiss my cheek.

We all packed into another Uber and arrived at The Partition a few minutes later. I loved the buzz of this bar. The music thumped through my chest as we entered. It was a sleek bar, contemporary with class. Low-key lighting and a plethora of alcoholic beverages to choose from. I let my eyes scan the crowd. Not overrun, but enough people to feel like it was a vibe. R n' B played in the background and a few people were already on the small dance floor toward the back.

"I got the first round, guys!" Rob put his hand up. Shauna bounced next to me at the bar and her curly locks came bouncing right along with her.

"I'm going with a mimosa. How 'bout you?" she said.

I scanned the menu. "Midnight in Paris. That's my pick."

"Ooo la la! I like, mamacita." I giggled and hugged her to me. Shauna was one of my dearest friends from campus and there was nobody I would rather party with. The music turned to a song by Pitbull. Rob started shaking his hips, which was a sight to see. He did have a little rhythm. Just funny, the way he spontaneously broke out like that.

"This is my jam! Come on, Celine, let's go bust a move on the dance floor," he yelled. He yanked Celine's hand and some of her drink spilled over. She just laughed. I shook my head at my friends. I needed to get warmed up first. Our exquisite drinks were prepared, and I dived into the first sip.

"Mmm, this is so good! Here, do you wanna do a swap?" I asked.

"Uh, no. I want all of my mimosa. Besides, you only took one sip. Damn!" she playfully retorted.

"Okay, girlfriend. I will have a Midnight in Paris all by myself." I clicked my fingers at her.

"I betcha you will be having one of those tomorrow after your date," she whispered cheekily. I raised my eyebrows at her.

"I'm not that easy. He's got to work for it. But he is one I would consider giving it up for a little quicker." I scrunched my nose and giggled. She sipped her cocktail and closed her eyes.

"Girl, he is finer than fine. You did good. So bold going up to him like that. I would never!"

"Had to. I couldn't let all that man just sit there without me saying anything. That's loco!" I said loudly. She slapped my leg in jest and drank.

"You right about that." We clinked our glasses together. Shauna slapped her hand on the bar.

"I knew it. Right in the middle of my drink. I gotta go pee. Are you okay here for a minute or do you want to go to the dance floor with the others?" she asked. We always looked out for one another when we were out. I eyed the bathroom. It was about ten steps away and I could see her and where everything was. Nobody that looked like a threat was around. People were low-key, chill.

"No. Go ahead. I'll be fine here. Don't worry. I can see you." I waved her to the bathroom.

"Scream if anything happens." We laughed together. It would give me time to see what was up. Nice beats. I could see Rob's head bobbing on the dance floor and they'd hit the strobe lighting. The DJ looked like he was setting up in the dance floor section. It was about to be lit.

"Hello, mamacita. You looking real good." An energy of darkness swam around me as a guy with dark eyes, a long nose and leather jacket rolled up on the right of me at the bar. My pace of breathing shot up instantly. His eyes put me off. His smile was sleazy. I froze for a minute.

"Hey." I clammed up and my face dropped. *Shit.* I should have moved when Shauna asked.

"Are you here with friends?" the guy asked. His looks resembled a snake. He bent in a little too close, with no regard for my personal space. His rancid breath was close to my face. I pulled my head back a little.

"Yeah. I am, in fact. They're right over there and my other friends will be here any minute." I raised my voice to get him to leave and pointed to the dance floor. He didn't take the hint. His strong cologne made my throat tickle came up.

"Interesting. So you like to fuck or what?" He spat out the question with force. He had an accent. I shot up out of my seat and splashed the drink on his face. Angry eyes leered back at me and the guy stuck his tongue out in a lecherous way. He wiped the water off his face with his sleeve. The bartender was at the other end of the bar and serving drinks.

"Get away from me, you asshole!" I yelled vehemently. He let out an evil husky laugh.

"I take that as a yes. Let me get you another drink." I watched the bathroom door. *What the hell is Shauna doing in there?* Before I knew it, another guy came from the other side of me. I saw his hand only. I was busy dealing with the ugly cretin in front of me. On the inside webbing of his finger was a teardrop. That was all I saw. I was boxed in and couldn't get out. My body went into lockdown and I felt frantic. The guy on the right was practically trying to straddle my knees. If you looked from the outside, my head was covered. Rob wouldn't be able to see me. *Fuck.*

"Move, you asshole!" I shouted and pushed his shoulder out of the way so I could be seen by the public. The music had stepped up a notch since the DJ was playing. The bartender looked at me from the other end when he heard a loud voice. The guy tapped his friend behind me.

"Come on, let's go," he said.

"Hey! Leave her alone!" the bartender shouted and rushed to my end of the bar. The sleazy snake waved at him.

"No harm, no foul. We leave now." The guy spoke with a thick European accent. I held my throat as a tear trickled down my face. Shauna floated out of the bathroom and her face turned cold as she locked eyes with mine. The guy flicked his long pink tongue out at me as I watched him walk out the door. The other guy was dressed all in black and looked like a full roll of dough. Dark hair and dark glassy eyes like the other guy. I couldn't get the teardrop out of my mind. It seemed significant.

"Babe, are you okay?" Shauna tracked my eyes to the door and saw the back of the two dudes. Her instinct made her angle to move to them. I pulled her arm back.

"Don't. Please don't. They look dangerous."

The bartender looked at me with concern.

"Do you want me to call the cops? Seriously, what did he say to you?" he asked, angry.

"Just a sleazebag. Nothing I want to repeat." Celine and Rob were still on the dance floor and hadn't seen what happened. Shauna put her arms around me.

"Do you want to go? What do you want to do?" Shauna pressed.

My hands were trembling as I tried to gather myself and think. "The guy had a gang symbol, I think, on the inside of his hand."

Shauna's eyes widened. "Holy fuck, that's crazy."

I chewed my bottom lip from nervousness. "I'm scared to go outside. What if they're out there? Shit."

Shauna tightened her grip on me. "I don't think they're hanging around," she said. Shakily, I reached inside my purse and texted my brother. The bartender, seeing I was okay, served a few other customers.

"Hey bro can you come pick me up?"

"Are you ok? Now?"
"Yes now"
"Ok be there in 5"

I sensed Palo would know who they were. That symbol. The guy's eyes looked like death. Like he had no soul. There had been scratches all over his fingers and he smelled heavily of cigarettes. Palo came and picked me up and I left the others there together. Shauna wanted to come with me.

"No, stay. Have fun for me. I just have to go home now. I can't be here." We hugged and I walked out of the club and ran to Palo. We sat quietly for a while and he looked at me with concern in the car.

"What happened?"

"Two guys tried to close in on me at the bar. I couldn't get out," I relayed.

"What the fuck?" I watched my brother's face turn to a dark cloud. "Where were your friends?"

"They were there, but it all happened so fast. Do you know anyone with a teardrop on the inside of their finger?" I watched as we turned in the driveway. Palo's face turned white like a sheet. He went deathly quiet.

"Palo, talk to me! Do you know them?" I asked, exasperated.

He housed silent anger. I could sense it. He cricked his neck. "What were they wearing? Let's go inside and you can describe them to me."

Now I felt scared. Palo dropped his keys on the table as I sat down.

"Sit, tell me, sis." Palo's stern voice let me know he meant business.

"One of them was kind of weedy, wearing black and his eyes were dark. He had a long nose. The other one was fat and wearing black. He had the teardrop between his fingers."

Palo got up from the seat he sat in and came back with his phone.

"These guys?" He showed me a group picture of Las Balas and pointed to them. One was kneeling in the photo and the other one was standing off to the side.

"Shit! That's them. Yes." My body tensed up as I recognized them. Palo balled up his fist, his lip forming a hard line. He truly looked like he was going to punch a hole in the wall.

"You're proving my point! This is why I didn't want you becoming president." I flailed my arms around.

"Shhh, relax! I got it handled. This is exactly why I need to be president. Don't ask me no more questions!" he spat back. He drove his index finger into the marble table. Perplexed and worried, I looked at him.

"Palo, what do you mean? What are you going to do? Did they know I'm your sister?"

Palo was already walking away from me. His voice traveled as he walked. "Of course they did, motherfuckers!"

El Diablo was dead, but he was still haunting everybody from beyond the grave.

DIEGO

Cogs were turning in my mind and my whole operation was moving in the right direction. I found a sweet little place off Santa Fe Drive.

Another glorious sunshiny day in Cali and a new goal to scout the hotspot for a repair shop. Time to get this chapter going.

Ryder rang through. "Hey, my man. How are you settling in? Things okay up there?"

"Real good. Merced is shaping up real nice. I'm checking out a warehouse shortly," I said.

"Okay. Nice work. If you need any connects up there, let me know. Watch your back; the Las Balas crew run out of Merced. We ain't been cool with them for a minute."

"I hear you. I'm laying low. I haven't seen or heard anything," I responded.

"All right. Nothing major my end. Just a check-in."

"Definitely, I expect nothing less. Hook up with you soon. Bye, Ryder."

"Peace."

I rode out the back of Merced. The warehouse had

popped up in the classifieds so I made it my business to go check it out. Brown specks of dust flew up from the road as I turned into the place. A good-sized warehouse. Windows on all sides and solid aluminum. I got off the bike and peeped inside. I tapped the glass. Concrete floors inside, great for what I needed.

"Hello, Diego, is it?" I heard a professional voice behind me as I looked in. A lady in heels and a corporate outfit showed up.

"Hi, Sue, right?"

She cast her greedy eyes over me. Oh. She wanted me. *I might be able to charm her into a discount.*

"Is that name Spanish?" she breathed.

"Yeah. Argentina." I grinned.

"Nice." She cleared her throat. *Okay-looking if you're into the housewife type. Not for me.* "Okay, so let's go in. This place used to be an aircraft hangar. It's perfect for a business that would house cars, planes, machinery, something of that nature. Has all the trimmings. Basins, toilets, a breakroom. Everything. Feel free to take a look around. Lemme know if you have any questions."

She sold the place to me and all with a salacious smile. I had that effect on women for some reason.

The place was spacious. I could visualize where the bikes would go and how many I could handle as a repair shop. I would need to install a couple of things. I checked the sliding garage doors at the front. A large padlock. She preempted my next question.

"The warehouse has an alarm code installed, of course. This feature was added by the previous owner." I nodded and assessed the situation, then took some photos so I could picture where to set up everything.

"Okay, thanks, I appreciate it. Think you could negotiate on the monthly price?" She licked her lips blatantly. All that did was make me think of Misty's lips. Not long to go before I saw her fine ass again.

"I don't know what you have in mind, price-point wise?"

I closed the gap between us and licked my bottom lip, giving her my bedroom eyes. "I was thinking a fifteen-percent drop since I would have to re-install the windows at the back. A few of them are cracked." I had her weak at the knees. If I was bored, I might have taken it a little further with her. But I didn't because all I had on my mind in the way of women was Misty.

"Umm, I mean...I can take it back to the owner and let's see."

"Would you? That would be great." I touched her arm. Just a little sealer for the deal. Her mouth formed an O and shifted to a smile.

"Okay. I'll see what I can do. I will let you know tomorrow."

Pretty good site overall and ideal for the shop. I left satisfied with the outcome. I shot off a couple of texts to Misty and hit the sack for the night.

Morning daybreak rose and my body clock kicked into gear, letting me know what time it was. I looked over at the alarm clock. Saturday. A day trip with Misty. By the time I got breakfast in, showered and shaved, it was time to head over to pick up the Puerto Rican babe. For some reason, she didn't want me picking her up from her house.

"Can you meet me in the parking lot of McDonald's again?" she asked nervously.

"Sure. But I got no problem picking you up from your house. I don't have to come inside," I responded.

"Uh, some other time. McDonald's today."

"Okay, suit yourself."

I spotted her car and she jumped out. I was on my bike and had the second helmet in hand. I owned a car, but I couldn't remember the last time I drove it. My bike was the only thing I needed. Even in hiking shorts and boots she gave me a hard-on. She didn't skip a beat as she put her arms around my neck and kissed me full on the lips. *What's a man to do?* I reciprocated the hell out of that kiss. Her lips were hot and tasted like fire. She smelled like she was fresh out of the shower.

"Hi." I licked my lips. "That was a hell of a greeting."

Her cat-like eyes twinkled back at me. "You didn't like it?" she responded smugly.

"Oh no. Don't be mistaken. I'm very happy with the greeting." I handed her the helmet. "You ready to hike with me?" I cut to the chase. I figured we would get to the get-to-know-you stage when we got to Yosemite Park.

"Yup. I'm ready."

I patted the back of my seat.

"Okay, hop on back, lil' mama." We rode for about an hour and a half to Yosemite Park, taking in the scenery along the way. Misty's warm hands around my waist felt good. *Me and a hot girl on the back of my bike. Yeah, life is good.*

Yosemite National Park. Like stepping right into a fantasy world. Rusty red and blue mountains lined the back of the park with their jagged ridges. In the foreground, the park was surrounded with trees of all varieties. The park made us look like toothpicks in the grand scheme of things.

"Wow, this is incredible!" Misty exclaimed as I parked the bike.

"You've never been here before?"

"No. I haven't. So crazy. I've lived in Merced for the last ten years and I've never ever been here," she gushed. She spun around, captivated by the park. Made me smile to think I could bring her a new experience. Helmets were off and we were ready to hike. The roar of the waterfalls made my ears perk up.

"Can you hear that? If I knew they had waterfalls here, I would have brought my shorts to swim."

"That water would be ice cold. You would get hyperthermia and then I'd have to revive you."

Misty laughed. I grinned back at her. I grabbed her hand and held it as we walked to check out the trails.

"I wouldn't mind that at all. Not one bit," she laughed. I kissed her hand as we reviewed the trails. "We're going for the easy trail, right?" She glanced at me.

"Yep. I'm not trying to kill you. I just thought this might be nice, and not boring."

She inhaled a deep breath. "It's definitely not boring, that's for sure."

We picked the trail we wanted to walk and I handed her a bottle of water.

"I don't want you falling out on me," I told her.

"I won't. Promise." California blue skies all the way around. A familiar bird call rang out. One I knew. I looked up to a circling eagle above the pine trees. "Wow. This is the best. Thank you for bringing me." Misty looked up at the sky right along with me.

"You're welcome." I squeezed her hand. The gravel from the trail crunched underneath our feet as we admired wildflowers and cute squirrels along the way. "So you said you've been here for ten years. Where were you before that?" I enquired.

"I lived with my family in Mexico City."

"That's different. Did you like it there?"

"I mean, it was okay. I like it better here." She picked at a flower along the way and put it in her hair. A little Puerto Rican wild child.

"How about you, where are you from?" she asked. I decided to opt out about speaking on Outlaw Souls. I wanted the connection to be pure between us. We could get to the finer details later on.

"La Playa for eight years. Long time there." I glanced at her. She looked so free out here. "So, this morning you had me pick you up from McDonald's. Is that a precautionary measure? Have you got a man at home?" Direct bullet, shot straight. Misty swung her head to look at me.

"Nope. No man at home. I live with my brother right now and he can get a little funny." Was she telling me the truth? I'd been down this road before. Plus, she was a med student and ten years younger than me. I didn't want another Crystal situation on my hands.

The Cali heat started kicking in. When I'd looked at the weather beforehand it said mild-low sixties but the weather channel lied. My brow had beads of unnecessary sweat on it.

"So what's your brother do? Looking out for you, huh?" Turns out Misty was pretty fit. She was a few steps ahead of me. Fine by me; I got to watch her ass and to torture myself with lusty desire.

"Something like that. My brother works with computers and stuff. Likes bikes," she mumbled. "Catch up. Come on!" Her lithe body moved effortlessly as we walked farther on the trail. I didn't want to take her too far. Just enough so we could walk and talk. Get to know one another.

"He likes bikes? I like him already." Might be a chance to get him in the chapter. Although if I had no long-term interest in Misty, it could potentially blow up in my face.

"What about you? What are you going to do in Merced?" She puffed a little.

"I have a few things in mind. One of them I'm already doing." She eyed me suspiciously. Brought out a devious smile from me.

"What would that one thing be?"

My face feigned innocence.

"Oh. Only that I found a place. Accommodation. Let's stop here. Chill. I'm not trying to get fit or anything. I just wanted to do something different with you." I caught up with her and grabbed her from behind in a bear hug. If I wanted to crush her, I could. She was so lightweight. But that was not what I wanted. I just wanted to be near her. She had this tantalizing quality about her that I couldn't stay away from.

"I like that you did this. Even though you're ducking my questions," she said. *Okay.* We were playing a game.

"You're ducking too. You wouldn't let me pick you up from your house." She lifted her hair from the back of her neck. The heat and the walk made us both sticky. I handed her a water bottle.

"I told you why." She stepped back a little and surveyed me. "Don't you trust me?" she teased.

"Should I? I mean we just met. Takes time."

She guzzled down her water and looked around the park. We stopped in an open area and I sat on top of the park bench. Misty stood, stretching out her legs. I watched her closely. I hadn't realized how athletic she was.

"That's true. My brother can be overprotective so I want to just chill on it. He might start asking too many questions." Her cat eyes danced in the sunlight. I noticed the brown specks in them. So far, it sounded legit. I would let it drop for now. "What did you say you do again?" she asked. I set my jaw. *You can't talk, then I won't either.*

"I didn't. I'm just chilling right now. Nothing going." She raised her brows and cast her eyes to the mountain.

"Just chilling? What does that even mean? Are you retired or something? Are you doing something illegal?" Irritation laced her voice. I was getting under her skin. A little spice never hurt anyone. I wanted to bring it out a little.

"No. Illegal? Not my style. I'm just taking a break right now."

Her brow furrowed as she put her hand on her hip and glared like a lioness at me.

"What? Why won't you answer? You're not Ted Bundy, are you?" The indignity.

"Easy, easy. I surrender." I held up my hands in mock protest. "I'm into real estate and I'm looking for property right now, if you must know. I was just fucking with you."

"Ohhhh. Funny guy." I reeled her in to me so fast she almost lost her balance. She put her slender hand on my chest for balance. I grabbed the back of her neck as she turned in to me. Her arms stretched up around my neck. When I gazed into her eyes I knew I was stepping into a ring of fire. I took over her lips and divided them, our tongues gliding over one another. Her rapid breath chased mine. Heartbeats synced as one. I moved my hands to her ass, cupping it. A possession on my part. Both cheeks fitted right in my hand. If I was equipped we would have been making love in the wild. But I wasn't. To save us both, I pulled back. But my cock didn't; it stood to attention, ready for action. We both had to regain our footing, along with our breath.

"That was intense, papi," she murmured. I rubbed the back of my neck to let the fiery beast of lust die down.

"Uh-huh. I gotta tell you. You're sexy as fuck."

She bit her lip. "You've got potential." Her voice sounded like pure satin. She stared at my package and then back at my face on purpose. I broke out in laughter. Lil' mama had it going on. She was my type. Young and free in her expression. Problem was, did I want another young one?

"I do? Well, I'm happy to hear that. Let's head back," I said. We'd been out on the trail for over an hour. No point teasing myself or her and keep on walking. We mostly walked in silence. Both of us were dancing around one another with the questions. So I surrendered to enjoying the moment with her. We rode back into town and I dropped her off. We finished our morning with a few more kisses.

"All right, beautiful lady. I had a wonderful time with you. I will see you next time, right?"

"Yeah, you will. Call me." She winked and got into her car.

I left for my new home. It was sparse, but I had a few things delivered. I had my mind set on pizza and whiskey. My plans were interrupted by a phone call.

"Hullo. Miss me?"

Crystal.

"I could ask you the same thing, but since you're on my phone, I know the answer," I replied flatly.

"I wanted to, you know... See what was up. Can we talk, hang out?"

I sighed.

"I'm not in La Playa anymore. I got out." Silence.

"You left and didn't tell me?"

"Why would I? We weren't together anymore. Gotta let it go." Came off as callous, but she knew what time it was with me. I'd told her from the start. She wanted something I couldn't give her.

"Oh. Okay." The disappointment in her voice was apparent. "Do you want to see me?"

I paused. I cut things clean but it couldn't hurt, could it? I made an exception.

"Sure, come up here. But you know what it is. I'm not your guy like that." My stance was clear. Here came the women. Now I had two on my hands. One new and fresh and the other from my past. Things were about to get interesting.

MISTY

"We got a chapter meeting tonight. No. I don't care. Emergency meeting. Set it up." Palo's clipped tone sounded off in the house. He had the phone to his ear. A blond girl came out of his room and scurried like a mouse to the front door. I saw her on the walk into the kitchen. I rolled my eyes. *Another one.* My brother had chicas in rotation. As far as I knew, it was the same three. Looked like it was the blonde this week. I didn't know how he maintained all three. I had a full day of classes so I had to get in and out of the kitchen. I drank my coffee and ate fast. I wanted to talk to Palo first. This was the most we'd ever spoken. Normally, I kept away at the other end of the house.

"Palo!"

"Yeah."

"You wanna coffee?" My way to get him in the kitchen, otherwise he would make me go to him.

"Coming," he yelled. I took a sip of my coffee and waited. "Wassup?"

"What's going on with those guys from the club? You never told me."

"That's because I don't want you involved in anything. You got your studies to worry about." Palo rubbed his head again and looked down at the ground.

"Palo. Look at me." My voice was firm. "I need to know. I don't want to be in a position where I can't go out with my girls because of your fucking gang!" Palo massaged his hand and looked at me.

"Both of them are being taken care of. You're right, I should have told you. They were connected to El Diablo and I suspected them already. They were on my list to let go of. Now it's a little more personal because you're my baby sister and I ain't going to let nobody harm you." Passion permeated his voice. I waited for a beat.

"Palo. What aren't you telling me? Don't do anything stupid." I forced a cup of coffee into his hands. It nearly splashed out of the cup. He jumped back a little. I wanted him to know I was pissed.

"Watch it!" He steadied the contents of the cup. "Look. It's deeper than that if you want to know the truth. They were setting up a prostitution ring. Keep your mouth shut. I knew they were doing something but I didn't pick it up quick enough." My stomach tied up in knots. I wanted to vomit.

"Were they–" I started. Palo closed his eyes.

"Yes. I suspect they were. But I have enough evidence gathered to get them put away. I can leak some things to the police," he said.

"Are you fucking serious? I cannot believe you! You have to leave Las Balas." My blood pressure rose and was about to skyrocket.

"Calm down. Have I ever not protected you?"

"But–"

"Let me ask you again. Have I ever not protected you?" His eyes were fierce as he asked.

"No," I answered quietly.

"Then. Let it go. Go to your class."

"What are their names?" I wanted to know.

"No way in hell I'm giving you names! You're going to be nowhere near this."

"You involved me when you joined Las Balas, estúpido!" I didn't give him time to reply. I stormed out of the kitchen and swiftly grabbed my books. School would be my sanctuary now. I had to get out of my brother's house. I'd been there long enough. I got in my car and drove to school. My phone pinged. Palo.

"Don't be angry. It's handled."

Yeah. right. He would never leave them. I'd told him explicitly I wanted no part and now I was knee-deep in it. Because of me, a meeting was being called and two slime buckets were trying to use me for a pro' ring. *Disgusting.* I diced through the morning traffic, working to cut off time and be on time for class. But now to top it off I was going to be late. My mood-o-meter was on shitty now.

The phone buzzed again. I pressed the button for Bluetooth.

"Palo, don't even-" A pause.

"Palo? Should I be worried?" Diego's husky laugh entered my car.

"Ah- sorry. I was talking to my brother earlier. I thought it was him." Dead air sat between us for a minute.

"Okay... I wanted to hear your voice and say good morning." He skipped over it. I didn't want to discuss it anyway.

"Good morning." My mood-o-meter was right back up where it belonged. He'd called at the right time. I kept an eye on the traffic as it started to bottleneck. "What are you doing today?"

"I'm going to pick up the keys for a new property I've invested in."

Diego didn't strike me as the type of guy to be involved in

real estate. I'd learned over the years not to judge a book by its cover, however.

"Okay. What type of investment is it?"

"Hmm. It's a warehouse, a business," he replied calmly. I nodded my head.

"So have you always been doing that? How did you learn to ride bikes?"

"I've been riding bikes since I was a kid. I used to be in motocross. But it's brutal, so I switched to cruising on the open road."

"Oh really? I never knew that. Super cool."

"You look like you know how to ride a bike. Can you ride?" he asked.

"Yep. I can. My bro' taught me. I can ride a few types of bikes," I replied in a flirty tone.

"Ha! What? Did you say what I thought you said?" He sounded shocked. I wanted to see him, but I knew my schedule for school. I was staring down the barrel of some tough exams.

"Yep," I said proudly.

"You're ballsy. I like it."

"Of course. I'm Spanish."

"I'm aware, trust me. Know how to play pool?"

"Of course. I play at college sometimes. Why?"

"Pool, pizza, drinks? What do you think? Friday night if you're free," he suggested. The traffic eased up and I pulled into the college parking lot.

"Sounds good. Just call me with the details. I just pulled into school, so I gotta go."

"Okay, babe. I'll call you later in the week."

"Bye, papi."

"Haha. Bye."

Okay, better way to start the day. I had to hightail it to the C block in a hurry. By the skin of my teeth, I made it to the lecture hall. People were still talking among themselves. I caught the wave from Shauna and Rob.

"Hey, hey." I hugged them both and sat down. Shauna sat in next to me as usual.

"Miss Puerto Rico, you didn't respond to my text yesterday. You must be sick of me." She jokingly pouted.

"No. I'm trying to get my mind set up for these exams."

"You and me both. Are you okay after last week?"

My skin started crawling just thinking about those creeps.

"My brother knows them. He's dealing with it." Shauna knew some of what club my brother was in but she didn't know everything. I wanted to keep it that way.

"I was worried about you," she said. Mr. Sanders put up a slide with red blood cells on it. He was lecturing us on pathogens. I wanted to pay attention because I knew he was a hard marker. He dropped a lot of gems in his lectures.

"Okay. Now we've got everyone in. How are we all?" Mr. Sanders was a serious type of guy. White hair and thin with big dark glasses. They didn't suit his face, but oh well. He knew his stuff and had worked in a biochemistry lab for over a decade. Now he was head of the department at University of California. *Kudos.*

"Don't worry. I'm good. But I gotta move out. My brother is giving me the shits," I whispered.

"Oh, shit! Luckily, I like my roommate. What's going down with you and the hottie?"

"Well..." I smiled when I thought about those lips and those icy blue eyes. Oh, *and* the hair, his husky voice and that bike. "I'm taking it easy. I don't want to rush things."

Shauna shut it down quickly. "Are you serious? I would have rushed right in and taken off all my clothes on sight! The man is fine..." I widened my eyes at her. "Respectfully so. Respectfully. I ain't no man stealer." She quickly cleared it up.

"Yeah. I like him though. Let's see. I'm going with the

flow of it." Our talking got a little loud. Mr. Sanders gave us a look over his glasses. *Uh-oh.* A few people turned to look at us. I sank down in my seat and Shauna held back a laugh. I listened intently for the rest of the class. From time to time, Diego's penetrating eyes came into my mind. My whole body flushed with heat when I thought of where his mouth could go. I shook myself out of it. I had to focus. I had medical exams coming up.

As the day wore on, it got better. I took to looking at places to rent in between classes. The bonuses of staying with Palo were starting to wear off. I felt the taste of bitter resentment at his choices clouding me. The next couple of days flew by as I got back in the groove of studying and routine. Palo and I didn't speak. I just could hear his voice from time to time down the other end of the house. Friday night rolled around quick enough. I was in my room picking out an outfit with music on to set the mood, getting ready to meet Diego at the spot. I didn't want Palo messing up anything else for me.

I went with jeans, heels and an off-the-shoulder top. A little bit sassy but enough to get him worked up. Trouble was, I wanted to hold off, but my body said something else entirely. I walked out the door feeling good. I knew the place he was talking about, Kewl Cats. I drove over there and went inside. I did a doubletake when I saw him. Ripped jeans, tight thighs, a black T-shirt with an eagle on the back and tousled dirty blonde hair in a ponytail. The essence of badassery. I scanned the room. Casual place. Pool tables lined up in a row. Kind of dark lighting. Plenty of light over the pool tables though. A few of them were free. Groups of people and couples were playing. Pizza was being carried out to tables and making my mouth water. I saw Diego getting a drink at the bar. Of course I had to walk in a little later than the actual date time.

"Can I have one too?" I addressed him from behind his back.

He turned and his blue eyes pierced straight through to my pussy. I swear. I was turned on already and we hadn't even started talking. He put his drink down on the bar and lifted me off my feet with a kiss.

"Hey, sexy. Missed you."

I was on a high right now and this was fun.

"Missed you too. I've been working too hard. Let's have some fun."

"I agree." His eyes gobbled me up as I sat down next to him. He turned my chair toward him. "How are you?" He stroked his hand on my thigh and leaned forward for a passionate lip lock.

"I'm good now," I breathed. My plan to keep my legs closed might have been ambitious. One of my toughest assignments yet.

"I'll get you a drink. What will it be?" he asked. I licked my lips, reveling in the after-tingle of his kiss.

"A beer will be fine."

"My kinda girl." The guy was so hot it was incredible. I was aching from need inside. I looked at the pool table. I wanted him to shoot those balls off my naked body. I shook the fantasy from my head. Hard to stay sane with someone so hot. I wanted to look past that, though. I mean, what did I really know about the guy? Other than he was into real estate and rode a motorbike. My background with bikers wasn't so good. He came back a few minutes later with my beer.

"What are you drinking?" I asked, peering at the brown liquid in his glass. His blue eyes danced.

"Jack." *Fuck.* He really fit the stereotype of a biker. "Do you know how to play pool?"

"Hmm. A little, not much. Try not to blow me out of the water," I lied. Truth was I'd played pool a lot with my older brother. We had a pool table in our family home. I was a little rusty but still confident I had enough skills to hold my own. All eyes were on me and I liked it. I had his full attention.

"Okay. I'll teach you the ropes along the way. We can have fun with it." He sounded confident. The corner of his mouth twisted and I knew what he was getting at.

"All right, cue up, sexy," I said. I grabbed my cue from the rack and chalked the tip. I watched Diego's forearm as he did the same. "You can go first," I said in an innocent voice. I didn't want to give away my cards early.

"Okay, if you say so. Best of five to start with." I watched him rack up all the balls in a triangle. Strands of his blond hair hung in his face as he concentrated. He leaned forward and I took in the masterpiece. All hunk. I noticed a couple of females on the side, eyeing him as well. I couldn't be too mad. I would've gawked too. The balls responded to his force and scattered. The smalls went into the pockets first, three of them. Good start for Diego. "Looks like you're on bigs. Can you handle it?" He smiled. I blew the chalk off the top of my stick and lined up the table. *Play dumb for a while or play it straight. Hmm.*

"I was born ready, baby." I smiled.

"I hear you talking, let's see what you got." I turned up the heat a little. I had to walk past him to get the right angle on the ball I wanted to pocket. I strolled behind him and pinched his ass as I went past. It brought a smile to his face. I leaned forward, being sure to stand on my tiptoes as I lined up the ball I wanted to hit. I missed the pocket to the left on purpose.

"I know what you're doing," he said and I grinned at him.

"Is it working?"

"Yes. But that's not going to be enough to throw me off." He nibbled my ear on his way to his shot. An adrenaline rush of wanton desire hit me. *Okay. Time to up the ante.* This whole thing felt like foreplay. I watched as he pocketed two more balls. "You sure you don't want any tips? I can give you some pointers on that last shot," he said as his eyes searched my body.

"Sure, go ahead."

He stood behind me and grabbed the stick and my hands. I had to keep my breathing level. I was struggling.

"If you look at the ball through an eye-level view it will help you hit the target." I knew he was talking about pool but it didn't feel like it. The way I heard his voice was as if he was singing me a lullaby. His husky, rich voice sent shivers down my spine.

"Uh-huh. I got it," I said.

"Okay, go for it."

I poked my tongue out. Two balls were lined up vertically in the top left pocket. I leaned back and let my stick do the work. The bangs clinked two balls together as they rolled in one after the other.

"Seems my lesson paid off."

"Seems like it." His small was in the way of one of my bigs. I needed a diagonal hit. I bounced the white ball off the corner, knocked his out and my ball went in. Now his beautiful white teeth started flashing and he smirked.

"So it's like that, huh?" He flicked his tongue around the inside of his mouth and stared at me.

"What?" I shrugged. We had a little bit of an audience. Two other guys from another table saw my shots and were watching from afar. Pizza came out to our stool table. Diego pointed to the slices.

"You know what... Wanna slice before I kick your butt?"

"I mean, sure." I sauntered around the table and picked up a slice. The cheese dripped a little down my chin. Diego didn't waste any time scooping it up with his finger. I giggled.

"You're cute." He gave me a quick peck on the lips. "Still your turn. Do your worst."

"Oh, I plan to." I ran my fingers along the edge of the table and positioned myself. Time to show off. I placed the stick behind my back and perched on the edge of the table, knocking in another big. Diego closed his eyes and shook his head. Sound effects came from the background as I grinned.

"Ooo, she got you good, man."

Diego turned his head to the fan on another table. He groaned. "Don't encourage her."

The guy laughed. I was on a roll. I had two more balls on the table; one was a long shot. I bounced it off the left-hand corner, hoping it would connect with my purple big on the right. Missed it by an inch.

"Okay. No mercy now." He brushed past me; the white ball was right near my shoulder. "Are you moving or are you gonna stand there?"

I turned in to him; we were so close his breath was on me.

"How about no."

He let out a throaty chuckle.

"Okay," he breathed and I wanted to melt into the floor. He shot the ball straight past me and I heard it hit the pocket. "How about that now?" He grinned. I grinned.

I didn't end up winning. But it came down to the black ball so I gave him a run for his money, that was for sure. The end of the night came and I didn't realize the time, I was having so much fun. We packed up the pool table and headed out into the freshness of the California night. We strolled back to our respective cars hand in hand. Smiling together. I shivered a little.

"Cold?" Even in the dark, I could see the desire in his eyes.

"A little," I replied. We reached his car and he pulled me to him on the back of the hood. He cupped my ass and took

DIEGO

possession over my mouth. Hot, feverish energy ran through me and I wanted him to take it further. But my mind held me back. *Remember your promise to yourself. Take it slow.* I tunneled my hands through his hair. It was surprisingly soft. His three o'clock beard grazed my chin lightly. Took another minute before we surfaced for air. His arms were firmly wrapped around my waist and we were eye to eye. I was straddled between his legs.

"When can I see you again? Do you want to come to my place next time? I'll cook for you." His gentle sexiness hit my eardrum.

"Sounds good. I'd really like that."

"Good, come on, I'll walk you to your car." Not many people were in the parking lot and the lighting was dim. He saw me to my car safely and we kissed again before I slid in the driver's seat.

"I'll call you." He winked. I blew a kiss to him and started my engine. Now it was a game to see how long I could keep my legs closed.

DIEGO

Two weeks passed and I'd managed to sort all my furniture out and have it delivered to me. My chaise lounge and video games with my large flatscreen TV arrived. The bachelor pad was complete. I was now sitting in downtown Merced at the real estate office.

"Thanks, Sue. You've been great and I'm glad you managed to get that fifteen percent off for me."

She pursed her lips together and brushed me off. "No problem. It's been on the market a while, and we're glad to have a tenant in there." She smiled and moistened her lips. Oh yeah, she had the hots for me. I took a sneak glance at her legs. Not bad for an old broad. I signed the last of the paperwork and she handed me the keys to my new future. I'd already started advertising and ran a local ad for repairs in the paper. From my research, there didn't look to be too many bike repairs in town. I strolled out of the realtor's with a broad smile on my face. I rode straight over to the warehouse.

The first thing I did was run my fingers over the dusty windows. Nothing a little hose-down wouldn't fix. I unlocked

DIEGO

the padlock and switched on all the lights. My phone started to vibrate in my pocket as I moved around in the space.

"Hello, Diego speaking."

"Ah, yes. Hi. My name's Rick. I saw your ad in the paper for motorcycle repair. I've been waiting to get mine repaired. I got a lowrider, can I bring it in?"

I breathed a sigh of relief. Not that I was hurting for money but nobody wants to start off on the wrong foot in business. "Yeah, sure, bring it in. You'll be my first customer."

"Man. I'll be glad to. When you opening up?" His tone was urgent.

"Anxious to get her back on the road, huh?" I asked.

"Yes, I am. It's been a good little while. I want to take her out to the national park. Been dying to go. Me and a few fellas love that."

"Come in. I want to start getting a few rides together, now I'm in town too. I'm part of a club called Outlaw Souls. I don't know if you've heard of them." I figured I would recruit via word of mouth. That would be the best way to get the chapter on track.

"Small world after all. I got a cousin who's part of the La Playa chapter. Loves it. Says he should have signed up years ago," he chuckled.

"Rick, my man. We got a lot to talk about. Bring your bike by tomorrow. I'll be here from nine a.m."

"No problem. Look forward to seeing what you can do for her," he replied.

I didn't even ask him what the issue was. I knew I'd be able to fix it. I had my tools which I had shipped up. I used to fix bikes in my backyard when I was a kid. I remembered my time with my father.

"Hey, son, pass me that wrench over there, would ya?" Such fun memories. Dad and Mom had since retired to San Bernardino. Both of them were the wild and free hippie types. My father used to always say to me, "Let your soul be free, kid, let it be free."

My phone rang again. I didn't recognize the number on the screen. I answered as I surveyed what I'd need to get the place ready for business.

"Hello, it's your favorite retired stripper," a sultry tone said on the other end of the line.

I grinned. "Crystal, baby. How you doing?"

"I'm good. I wanted to take you up on your offer to hang out. I need to get away for a little bit anyway," she admitted. Guilt set in on me. I didn't for a million years think Crystal would actually come all this way to see me.

"So why are you calling now, Crystal?"

"I know. I just–" She stopped speaking abruptly.

I was leaning on the sink with my arms crossed, listening. "You just what?"

"Umm. I want to see you for old time's sake. I don't want anything from you. I just wanted to see if we could build a friendship somehow. I realize we're not together. Just a friendship, that's it."

She rambled on as I looked down at the scuff of my biker boots. The laces were undone. That was how I liked them. "Look. I'm seeing somebody now and if you're coming up here, you gotta know that. So just chill when you get here," I said firmly.

"Awesome. You can tell me all about her. I want to tell you what I'm doing now. I can't wait to see you! How does your calendar look in a couple of weeks? We can do brunch."

I smiled. Her bubbly nature was always one of my favorite things about her. "Okay, Crystal. You're on. I'll take you to a cool burger spot. You'll like it."

"Awesome. See you, Diego."

I hung up and shook my head at the randomness of the call. Just as I was about to change clothes and get to work cleaning up the place, Ryder's number popped up on the phone.

"Hey, Diego. I wanted to be the first to congratulate you," his rich deep voice boomed. Ryder was the epitome of a rider, a muscular, proud man with a strong profile and real presence. He was the right man to lead the charge at Outlaw Souls.

"Thanks, Ryder, so far, so good. I met a guy today who's bringing his bike in tomorrow. He's interested in the chapter. I didn't catch the name but he has a cousin who's part of La Playa."

"That's great news. Listen, I was talking to the guys in the last meeting. We want to come up there and support. Help you get some movement going. We thought we might do a community opening and introduce ourselves. What do you think? If we come up there in a few weeks, would you be ready?" Ryder asked.

"That timing would be good. I'm confident I can get a few things moving by then as well."

"I know you can. I haven't taken that ride up there for almost a year, would you believe. Might ride along the coastline," Ryder mused.

"I wish I rode the coastline. I'm kicking myself," I said.

"Yeah, you should have, it's real pretty. Next time though. It's not going anywhere," Ryder advised.

"For sure. I'm here in the warehouse right now, cleaning up and getting things set up."

"Okay, great. We got some funds in the kitty for those platform lifts you need. Invoice the club for them and purchase on the credit card I gave you. We raised the funds from the community drive last year," Ryder said.

"Okay, done. I'll get that up tomorrow and shoot you an email."

"Sweet. And good job, Diego. We're happy to have you as part of the chapter."

"Me too. I'm loving it here."

"Glad to hear it. Take care 'til next time."

"You too. Thanks, Ryder." Once the phone clicked off, I set to work wiping down benches. There was one platform bench already set up, but I would need a whole lot more. It already had built-in shelving, so I just needed to fill it. As one person, I could only do what I could. Once a few more people came on board I could hire a couple of guys or they could volunteer and help out. My mind drifted to Misty. It hadn't been that long since I'd seen her, but my mind kept thinking of her. I'd called her a few days ago.

"Hey, sexy man," she'd answered.

"Right back at you, minus the man part," I said. "Is there anything you don't like to eat? I wanted to see when you're free for dinner at my place."

"Can we do mid next week? These exams coming up have my nerves frazzled."

"C'mon! You're gonna ace it. I know you will. I'm not taking no for an answer. So anything you don't eat?"

"Ok yeah, sorry. Maybe a break from studying will do me good. My mind is just a bit scattered right now. I'm in the library. No. I'm a meat eater, nothing too crazy but I'll eat anything... I have a Spanish appetite."

"Good. I'll surprise you then."

"Wow. I didn't know you could cook. You get points for that," Misty said.

"Oh, do I? I hope I can get a few more points with you." My bold response made her laugh.

"Haha. We'll see. I gotta go to class right now. But I can't wait to see you."

"Me too. Bye, mamacita."

"Mwah."

As I hit the backstreets of Merced to my apartment, I felt like I'd done a good day's work. I got in the door and grabbed

DIEGO

a well-deserved beer from the fridge. I guzzled it down and prepared to hit the shower. Misty was arriving in a couple of hours. My apartment was neat and there were no things I needed to take care of. I liked space and clear areas. I wasn't a messy dude. I showered and got all the ingredients out for the recipe I wanted to impress Misty with. I turned on some soft melodic music to set the mood. I breathed easy as I retrieved the bowls and plates for preparing the ingredients. The dish of the evening was shrimp carbonara. I had on a fresh navy blue collar shirt with the sleeves rolled up and jeans with bare feet. I even ran the brush through my hair. It stayed blonde on top because of the California sun. In winter it turned a few shades darker. I cut my beard down to a number one. I was almost clean-shaven.

The doorbell rang a couple of hours later and I sang out, "Speak now or forever hold your peace." No sound came from the other side. "Hello?"

"Well, you said forever hold your peace. It's Misty," she replied jovially. I opened the door and a goddess stared back at me. I breathed in her soft perfume. Her thick auburn hair framed her face and hung level with her breast line. Her denim jeans hugged her curves in the right places and her tight white top shone in the dark. She fingered her gold necklace as she waited to be invited in.

"Damn, you look good," I said with a wooden spoon in my hand.

She pointed to it and stifled a laugh. "So do you with that spoon in your hand."

I hid the spoon with one hand behind my back, leaning forward to kiss her. "Come in, beautiful."

She entered and looked around, sniffing. "Hmm, something smells fantastic. I'm a foodie so I'm excited about what you're cooking."

"Might not be what you think. No Spanish flavors

tonight. I'm cooking shrimp carbonara. Any objection to carbs?" I asked, skimming my eyes over her body.

She returned the favor. "Nope."

"Can I get you a drink? Do you like red wine?" I asked nervously.

"Yes I do." I poured her a glass and she continued to look around my apartment.

"Go ahead, take a look around. I'm putting on the fettuccine now and stirring the sauce."

"Okay." She scooped up her glass and moseyed through the rooms. She returned a few minutes later, sitting at the kitchen island in front of me. "Are you going to decorate a little bit? It's kind of bare."

I let my eyes linger on her. "I will. I have a few photos of my parents I want to put up. Plus a few other motorcycle posters I have to get out of boxes."

The water bubbled as the fettuccine came to the boil. "Can I help you with anything?" She licked her lips and it made me want to taste them again.

"Yes. You can chill out and enjoy your wine. You're my guest and I want you to have fun." Amusement played in her eyes.

"Okay." She twisted the bottom of her wine glass in her hands. Even her long slender hands were sexy.

She propped her hand underneath her chin and continued scanning me. I spoke as I watched her right back. "Any patient you have will be in trouble."

She frowned. "What makes you say that?" She sat up a little straighter.

I turned to her from the sink and looked her in the eyes. "Because you might cure them of one thing, but how will you cure them from heartbreak?" I grinned.

She threw back her head with laughter. "Mr. Funny Guy is back again. That was the corniest line ever."

"Yeah, but it worked. You're laughing," I retorted.

"That's true. Good point."

"Not long now. I just gotta fry up the shrimp."

"Okay," she replied chirpily. "I'm enjoying the wine. It's smooth. I like it."

"Thank you. I'm not too bad a pick with my wines." I pulled out my frying pan and sliced the knife through the butter, melting it in the pan. I sprinkled a little sea salt in, adding chopped garlic and laid down the shrimp, watching the pan sizzle.

"Can you smell that?" I sniffed. "Let the aroma hit you." I smiled.

She giggled and took a sip of her wine. "Smells *so* good."

I stirred in the rest of the ingredients and let the mixture simmer as I touched the tender pasta.

"Wow, I just noticed you laid out candles and everything. So sweet."

"Hey, I'm a sweet guy. What can I say?"

"So far so good," she responded.

"You're worth thinking of." I turned to see her reaction. She was playing with her hair, running her hands through it. Her magical mouth held a mysterious smile as she sipped her wine.

"Thank you. Let's toast."

"Good idea. Let's toast to new beginnings." We lifted our glasses in the air and clinked them together. Once I mixed all the ingredients for the sauce and drained the pasta, I plated up two dishes for us. "Plenty more if you want, so don't worry. My guests never leave hungry. Have a seat at the table, beautiful."

She moved to the table and waited as I placed the dish down in front of her. "Yum, yes, I can't wait."

I topped up her wine and finally sat with her. "Okay, now we're ready."

"Yes, we are."

"How's your last two weeks been?" I asked.

"I've been studying really hard. It's frying my brain, but I think I'm going to be okay." She curled the fettuccine around her fork and tasted. I waited. She closed her eyes and left a little cream sauce dripping from her chin.

We were sitting diagonally from one another, so I closed the gap. "Look at me for a minute."

She turned and I wiped her chin with my thumb and sucked the sauce off it. Her mouth dropped open as her eyes narrowed.

"You had a little sauce there," I told her huskily. I leaned back in my seat and took a bite.

"Umm. Thank you." She licked her lips and kept eating.

"It's amazing you're going to be a doctor. I can't study like that because I can't sit still. I like to build things. I'm more of a hands-on type of guy."

"I can see that." She glanced over my forearms. "So when did you start with the bikes and hey, by the way, what happened to the warehouse you went to look at?"

"Good memory. I got it and that's where I'm starting to repair bikes. I'm leasing it for now. I used to help my father repair bikes in his backyard. He played a huge part in that."

"Cool," she said with a smoldering glance that made my veins burn like hot coals. I watched her lips connect with the wine glass and sip. I felt a brushing sensation under the table. Misty's bare foot was sliding up and down my leg. I caught her leg mid-calf and kneaded a little.

"Mmm," she moaned, closing her eyes.

"Feel good, baby?"

"Real good." Her sensual gaze met mine as we left our plates and I pulled away from the table. She moistened her lips and her chest began rising and falling. I beckoned her to come sit on my lap. She straddled me and wrapped her legs around the chair. Her silkened locks smelled of fresh shampoo as I pushed them back from her face. Her slender arms slid into the back of my hair.

"I love your wild hair," she murmured.

"Thank you." I found an opening on her neck and kissed her there lightly. She parted her lips in desire. I focused on the fullness of her lips as my hands cupped her buttocks. I slid her forward so we fit together tighter. Chest to chest, hearts beating together. The soft melodic mood music in the background only heightened the magic of the moment. I took over her lips, prising them open and tasting their velvety fire. Our tongues danced as one. She arched her back and moaned in pleasure as I fondled her breasts. The assault of kisses to her neck made her buck against me, letting me know she was ready for more.

"Misty. I want you," I growled, my manhood rising from primal desire. Her olive-green eyes sparked with Spanish fire.

"Then let's go." She nibbled my ear as I lifted her straight up from the chair and carried her to my bedroom. She laughed with glee and it made me smile.

"You're so sexy. I swear to God."

"So are you, papi."

I swiftly strode to the bedroom and let her slide down from my hands. She unbuttoned my shirt with her slender fingers as I lifted her top out of her pants. I worked out of my jeans and she started to take hers down.

"Wait, let me." I pulled them down her legs as she shifted backward on the bed in her g-string. She signaled with her finger and I crawled on top of her like a hungry lion ready for his feast. I could barely suck in enough oxygen from the internal fire I had for her. She splayed her hands across my chest as I nibbled down her neck. She shivered from my touch, very responsive. I unclipped her bra and bent my head to suck and lick her swollen buds. I circled there for a moment until I felt both had been satisfied. She cried out in delight and lifted her body for more. I stroked her stomach as I kissed all the way to her belly button, pausing there and circling with my tongue. My cock strained under the fabric of my underwear, but I was more interested in Misty's pleasure first. I slipped her out of her g-string and placed my fingers into her hot entry door to paradise, to check the temperature. She gasped in shock and parted her ocean for me to dive into. Misty was hot. moist and ready for me. She tunneled her fingers into my hair as I caressed her inner thigh with my lips. She writhed in frustration as I stayed there for a minute.

"You're teasing me," she moaned with primal urgency.

"Hold still." I parted her with my tongue and slid my hands under her buttocks for maximum entry. I let my tongue flutter and move more gently. At first I increased the pressure and drove my tongue deep inside her flower. Just when I thought she wouldn't be able to take it anymore, I located her most sensitive spot and began the slow flicking of my tongue, sending a torpedo of an orgasm rippling through her body. Her eyes were closed tight and the sweet release made her call out.

Her feline eyes opened with dark eroticism as I stepped out of my underwear. My erection stood full mast. I reached to my side drawer for a condom and rolled it on quickly. Misty's eyes widened with feverish desire. I lifted her legs to my shoulder, holding her feet. I gave her ankle a passionate love bite and she moaned. I penetrated her sleek walls, finding a solid rhythm as her breasts bounced in time with the impact. Her breath was out of control now as I thrust into her hot furnace. Her primal Spanish fire charged as she pushed her buttocks against me and bit down on her lip and guttural sounds came out. More friction, more heat and sweat beads covered us both.

"*Harder, papi!*" she groaned with desperation. I leaned over her, grabbing her buttocks and driving deeper and faster. She pulled my hair with one hand and I pinned the other. It was impossible to hold on to control as her face contorted with ecstasy and an explosion ripped through my cock, taking me over the edge. Misty's cries rang out with mine simultaneously as I felt her internal walls clamp down around me in orgasm. I lay on top of her with a raspy breath, eventually rolling off, seeing stars on the ceiling. She stroked my chest with the back of her hand.

"Just what the doctor ordered," she cooed. We both laughed as I scooped her to me, kissing her cheek.

"You're so wonderful, Misty," I said quietly.

She lifted her arm around my head and stroked. "So are you," she murmured, and we fell asleep in each other's arms just like that.

MISTY

Merced, the place known as Our Lady of Grace. If it wasn't for my studies I'd be somewhere else. But lying in Diego's bed, I knew Merced was the place I needed to be for now. Light streamed in the window behind us as I nestled in the crook of Diego's arm, dozing peacefully. He woke me up with a kiss.

"Good morning, beautiful," he said, stroking my bare back.

"Good morning." I shielded my eyes under his arm, not wanting to get up. He showered me with kisses, curling his arm around me. I giggled. "Noooo, I don't wanna get up!" The sound of the radio alarm clock came on and Diego reached with his free hand to stop it.

"Baby, don't you have to go to class this morning? I can't let my doctor be late for class."

I groaned in irritation a little more as I stayed in the fetal position, reveling in the comfort of the bed. I was feeling too floaty to go to class. Diego was up now and looking over my face.

"You look gorgeous with bed hair." He put a finger underneath my armpits and started the tickling assault.

My eyes widened. "Noooo, what are you doing! That's not fair. I like it here, this bed is nice." I snuggled my face into it and sighed.

Diego tugged the sheets from under me, letting the cool air hit my naked skin. "Not like you can't come back. I know you have class because you told me. I'll make you a strong cup of coffee and some toast, how about that?"

"I guess..." I started the slow movement of getting up. Diego already had shorts on and was watching me as I rose.

His eyes wandered over my body. "I can't stay in here too long, otherwise we won't make it out of this room."

I laughed. "Uh-huh. I won't argue with you there. I'm going to take a shower."

He tapped my butt lightly. "Fresh towels are on the rack, baby. Coffee coming up."

Diego's dirty blond streaks hung over his face as I admired his masculinity. The guy was sexy. His broad, tanned shoulders made me feel safe. On the walk out, I noticed the large eagle tattooed on his back. No other visible tattoos were on him. I made a note to ask him what it represented.

I showered and let the hot water wash the remnants of lovemaking from me. Feeling invigorated and refreshed, I made my way to the kitchen. The sunlight from his open windows made me squint.

"Hey, hey. Here's my girl. I got a nice cup of coffee for you coming up. How you like it?"

I saw it was percolated coffee. "Just black with a little milk is good. What time is it? Gotta be early," I remarked.

"Yep. It's seven a.m."

I smiled at him as he poured a cup and put it in front of me.

"You're really thoughtful, you know that? You could have

let me be late..." He turned to me and leaned across the kitchen counter.

"I keep trying to tell you, I'm a nice guy." I grinned and sipped my coffee. "I have to get to the garage this morning as well. I'm fixing my first bike," he said with pride.

"Wow. That's good. I thought you were more into real estate for some reason?"

He paused for a second and sipped his own coffee.

"Sure I am, but I fix bikes too and it will help me get people to the chapter I'm opening."

I froze for a minute and sat my coffee down. "Chapter?" I frowned. "What do you mean 'chapter'?"

"Toast?" he asked.

"Yes. I'll have a couple of pieces. Chapter? Tell me more." My stomach started to tighten up. I had a feeling I knew what he was about to tell me.

He took the bread out and put it into the toaster. "So, I'm part of a motorcycle club called The Outlaw Souls and we've decided to expand the chapter here in Merced. I'm heading that up right now."

He faced me with earnestness in his eyes and I knew my face was flushing red. Silently, my insides were churning at the news. I felt the disappointment wash over me.

"Are you serious? You're part of a motorcycle chapter and you didn't think to tell me?" I spat back dramatically.

A look of confusion came over Diego's handsome face. "What's the issue, baby? I mean, I ride bikes. It's no different being in a club than you being part of a club – I don't know, to do with doctors or something."

I sat up straighter and looked him dead in the eye. "Like hell it is! Outlaw Souls? What kind of title is that? We live in Merced, this place has the highest crime rate in California. You're lying right now." My blood was boiling, mainly at myself, but I wouldn't tell him that.

He eyed me with interest as he moved closer to me. I stood up from the chair, even though only half my coffee was finished. My hands were trembling with anger.

"I like that feisty Spanish fire in you," he said. "You need to calm down though. This club is about community. We do a lot of great things for people. Starting a chapter in a place with crime is actually a good thing."

I crossed my arms and looked back at him. "I don't want anything to do with shadiness. I know about motorcycle gangs. I just don't need that in my life, Diego."

He closed the gap between us, completely wrapping his arms around my waist. His eyes darkened as he looked into my eyes. "Sweet thing, I wouldn't put you in danger like that. I'm telling the truth. I hear where you're coming from. But stop worrying. We're legit, I promise you that."

I felt the knot start to unravel part way. I circled my finger around his chest and he smiled at me with those delicious eyes. Hard to resist the man. He didn't know what I knew, though.

"Look- I just. I don't know. I want to be a doctor so bad and look after my community. I can't jeopardize that."

He stroked my back as his warm breath fell on me. "So you're telling me something…"

Puzzled, I talked into his chest without looking up. "What do you mean? I don't understand."

He smoothed down my hair as the toast popped. "Are you talking about a future with us?"

I blushed. "I mean- no. That's not what I meant. We're not together officially, I get it. I just don't-"

"I'm not exactly against the idea if you can't tell." He grinned at my anxiety. "You've got nothing to worry about and I would never want to put you in harm's way."

My mind began to race. "What's to stop a rival gang approaching you, though? You might be doing good, but how do you know they are?" My heart was beating faster than I wanted it to.

He released me. "Want your toast? How do you like it?"

He was changing the subject and it was ticking me off. "Please answer me, and no, all of a sudden I've lost my appetite." I started packing my purse and getting things ready, looking around to make sure I didn't forget anything.

He ran his hand through his hair. "Yes, we may have had some dealings with other motorcycle clubs in the past. But that shit's in the past. I would tell you, just like I told you now. We do a lot for our people and we want the community involved. Just give me a chance," he pleaded.

I closed my eyes briefly. "Look, we're good, you just shocked me with it. I didn't know that's what you were into. Like you said, I gotta get to class, plus I have to go home first. Thanks for the toast, but I'm going to leave it." My flat tone gave it away.

"You're not good completely, though, are you? I can hear it in your voice..." he challenged me and I avoided his gaze. "Don't turn away from me now when we're just getting started. Give me time to show you, mamacita."

I sighed. "I need some time to think about it, Diego." I softened and went to him standing on my tiptoes, giving him a quick peck on the lips. I walked quickly to the door, opening it.

He stood there in disbelief. "I can't believe you're just going to leave it like this. Over me opening a bike club? There's got to be more to this... Don't walk out." His eyes were begging for answers.

"Diego," I said as I turned back one last time. "I had a wonderful time last night. I enjoyed myself and you. I just need a little time to think it over. I'll talk to you soon."

"Well, I mean, okay. You'll see. Not much I can do if you won't listen to me," he mumbled.

"Bye, Diego." Fuming, I headed to my vehicle. The California air felt a little colder today. I put my hands on the wheel for a minute, contemplating. *Have I been too harsh? Maybe his chapter is good. Am I letting my bias get in the way?* I cranked the engine, heading for home with these thoughts in my brain.

Lost in the daze on the drive home, I entered the house. Not a peep. My shoulders released. I didn't need Palo giving me shit. I went to my room and changed clothes quickly. I looked at my watch. I was making good time. I had class in two hours, plenty of time. I picked up my phone. Diego. He'd texted a bunch of love hearts to me. I couldn't help but smile. A bad boy softie. Who knew?

I switched on my laptop and googled Outlaw Souls. I scanned for pictures and information to see if I could sense anything or find something to incriminate Diego. I came across something that made my stomach lurch.

Outlaws motto: *"We stand united brothers in arms." "We are a law unto ourselves."*

The members were rough around the edges. Ten of them lined up with their backs facing the camera. Black motorcycle jackets with an emblem on the back. Another picture, Diego all smiles, flipping a burger on the grill surrounded by people. I scanned to the next picture. Bikes lined up in another and one person with a plume of smoke in the parking lot. I clicked out. I'd seen enough. I had to focus and get to class.

I drove through the traffic with my favorite Spanish tracks on in the car. I tapped my fingers and turned it up, trying to come to grips with the fact that I'd just slept with a guy from a motorcycle chapter. My brother rang on the Bluetooth as I drove.

"Hullo?" I answered.

"Ay. Are you all right?" he inquired.

"Yes, Palo, why wouldn't I be?" I replied with annoyance.

"I'm checking in as big bro', I wanted to let you know something too." Another reason for my stomach to tighten.

"Well, I'm good, what is it?"

"I've officially been sworn in as president and those two guys at the club will never bother you again."

Chills ran down my spine. "What did you do, Palo? What the fuck did you do?" I screamed, slamming my palms on the steering wheel. A lady to my left saw me and gave me a weird look.

"Calm down. I did what needed to be done. You just worry about school. Like I told you, we're going legit now, so get your emotions under control," Palo said calmly.

"Don't you tell me to get my emotions under control! I have to worry about you every day in that stupid gang," I yelled. The overwhelm pounding my chest was too much for me to bear. I wanted to pull over.

"We can talk later. I gotta go to work," Palo said sharply and clicked off. I closed my eyes for a moment as I sat at the lights. So much confusion swirled in my brain. What could I believe now? I pulled into the parking lot ten minutes later.

First up today was pharmacology; Shauna and I were paired up, working on a project. I texted her as I walked on campus.

"Where you at?"

"Cafeteria, before this dry ass subject."

"Lol"

Today the place looked bare as I crossed the manicured lawn to the square building in front of me. I spotted Shauna's curls before her and she was in line, picking up her coffee from the front counter. I approached sneakily.

"Boo!" She jumped and nearly lost her coffee.

"I'm going to kill you! If you made me drop my coffee there would be hell to pay." She kissed me hello on the cheek.

"I know. I have to get one too. Wait for me."

"How are you this morning? Ready for Mr. Dry-ass Stewart and his pills?"

I shook my head at her with a downturned mouth. "I don't know how I am. I saw Diego last night and he's into some things I didn't know he was into..." I ordered my coffee and waited.

Shauna's eyes lit up as bright as her yellow hoodie. "Ooo! Girl, tell me everything! So he really is a badass?"

"Thank you," I said to the cashier while he handed me my coffee. I walked with Shauna as we headed to class. "I never said that. I just don't know that I want to be associated with it all."

She gave me a strange look. "You're being cryptic. What does that mean?"

We headed up the stairwell to Block C. "He's part of some motorcycle chapter and he says it's a good one. I've never known a motorcycle chapter to represent anything good," I blurted out.

"Ohh, so you don't know if you can trust him yet," Shauna answered.

"Something like that. I guess it takes time and I don't need that shit right before those exams." I huffed as we reached the top of the stairs. "Damn, those stairs nearly killed a bitch."

She laughed as she opened the stairwell door. "You and me both. Might be kind of cool though to date an outlaw. Plus, I can hear the goss'!"

I shook my head. "Girl, you are crazy. I knew I shouldn't have told you. And you pretty much hit the nail on the head. The chapter is called Outlaw Souls."

She rolled her eyes as we walked in the classroom. "Well, that's not predictable, much." We walked in single file as the classroom filled with students taking their seats. Mr. Stewart, a hefty man, nodded as we entered. "In all seriousness, if you feel uncomfortable, just take your time and see what comes. He might be legit, you know. You don't want to miss out on something great because you misjudged the guy."

"When did you become wise, Shauna? What happened?"

She shook her curls and shrugged her shoulders as we slid into two seats near the back. "Life, I guess."

Pharmacology was not my strong suit as I struggled to focus on the words Mr. Stewart said. Men and their motorbikes... Somehow I couldn't seem to escape them. Maybe I was the secret outlaw.

DIEGO

I texted her the love hearts. I didn't know what else to do. I threw the wasted toast in the trash and dumped the cold coffee in the sink. I stood at the sink for minutes, sipping on my coffee after she left. Shit didn't make sense. It was eight o'clock and my phone buzzed on the counter.

"Hello, Diego speaking."

"Hi, this is Courier Express, we are confirming pick-up delivery of two motorcycle platforms today. Will you be at the warehouse address of 34A Multon Road Merced between nine a.m. and five p.m.?"

"Yes, I will. Thank you."

"Great. We will see you then, sir."

"Okay." I bobbed my head. At least that part of my life had movement. I drained the last of my coffee and got ready to hit the road. I had a lot to do and a new client with a bike to fix.

Twenty minutes later after showering and heading over to the garage, Misty popped up in my head. Her sensual Spanish fire made me lick my lips at the memory, although it was marred by her anger in the morning. I opened up and paced the length of the garage. I pulled out the tool kit I had housed there and put down a stiff MDF board I found out the back.

I had deliveries in place for a new desktop computer to come, the raised platform for the bikes and now to confirm a few other things before Rick came through to pick up his bike.

"Morning, Ryder," I said.

"Hey, how you doing?" Ryder enquired in his full-toned voice.

"Alive and kicking," I replied.

"Good. Good."

"Hey, I need a few things, I need to stock up on parts. I want to confirm some parts with you."

Ryder coughed. "Excuse me, just woke up. Okay, so talk to me. I got news too. But tell me what you need first."

"All right, I wanted to run it by you before I send through the invoice."

"That's all right, that's what I told you to do. Hit me with it."

"I need a few torque wrenches, a chain breaker and riveter – just a few more depending on how the shop gets going. A hex set too, mine's in pieces. The platforms are on the way today, so thanks."

"Okay, that's not too bad. I got a few more customers for you. A couple of guys I know live up near Merced and I'm sending them your way. You're going to need these extras. We want to come up there this weekend, you game?"

"Hell, yeah. That will work."

"Okay, Diego. I'll let you get to it. Good job." Ryder's gravelly voice left the call. I had my coveralls at the warehouse and I put them on over my jeans and T-shirt. Time to get greasy.

DIEGO

Footsteps followed ten minutes later with two people. Both of them were males and they had bikes with them.

"Hey, Diego, right?" One called out from afar.

"That'd be me. We got two, huh?"

He smiled. "Yup. Once I realized you were part of Outlaw Souls I decided to bring my homeboy's bike in with me. This here's Derek."

He pointed to Derek as he stopped with the bikes and set their stands in place. I shook both their hands. Both mild-mannered, meek men. Nothing standing out about them.

"Hey, guys, nice to meet you both and thanks for your business. What's going on with them?"

Rick sighed as I looked the bike over. "I think I got a problem with the starter drive. I don't know. It's a common problem with Harleys."

I frowned and ran my fingers over the bike. "Yep. Might need a compensator kit. They're costly but it might be the answer. Leave it with me and I'll let you know."

Rick groaned. "I thought it might be that. This beast has cost me more than my house deposit."

I laughed at his plight. "That's a Harley for you. They cost money for sure. You have to really love them."

Rick put his hands in his pockets and rocked back on his heels. "You got that right. That's why I waited."

The other guy waited patiently, looking around the warehouse. "Pretty good spot for a shop. I got this dirt bike and it needs a service, nothing major like Rick here," Derek said.

I nodded. "Okay, great. If you guys can do me a favor and leave your name and numbers right here, I'll call you with the quotes. I may need to order parts."

"Appreciate it. I'll talk to you about the chapter when you get through fixing the bikes. I want to ask you some questions."

"Okay, no problem."

"Thanks, Diego, we'll leave you to it." I thanked both of them as they walked out. Confusion reigned in my mind still about Misty. I checked Rick's bike and decided to take it for a spin in the back parking lot. I wheeled it out and did a hard start and sure enough, a grinding noise began. Like I thought. I rang around for parts in the morning and then attempted to call Misty in the afternoon.

"Hi, you've reached Misty Narvaez and I'm not available right now. Please leave your name and number and I'll get back to you when I can."

"Hey, Misty, it's Diego. I just wanted to touch base with you. I'd like to invite you to meet some of the guys I ride with. I don't know if this will set your mind at ease about things. Anyway...I know you need your space and I respect that. Let me know what you think, either way."

Derek's bike was easier to work on and I had the service halfway done by lunch. I added a few extra things to it since it was my first time working with the client. I closed up shop at a reasonable hour and headed to my home with Misty's reaction still plaguing me.

The rest of the California week rolled into one, apricot skies rolled into blue and sometimes gray. Luckily, the weekend rolled around soon enough but there was still no word from Misty. In my dreams, I saw her kissing my lips and laughing. Even back when I was with Crystal, I didn't feel the passion I felt now for Misty.

Trainer, Ryder and Yoda were on their way to me and I was preparing to head to the workshop. I wanted to have the place looking great before they arrived. My phone vibrated on the counter as I made my way out the door.

"Yo," I responded.

"Hey, Diego! It's Yoda. Are you ready for us up there?"

"For sure. I'm glad the boys are on the way. I got the platforms and it's starting to shape up now."

"Sweet. Any ladies up there? What's the vibe? We might hit the town when we're up there. We're going to check into Studio 6."

I chuckled. "Yeah, there's some nice ladies up here for sure. You'll find something you like. The Spanish chicas are stunning."

Yoda laughed. "Sounds good to me."

I rode out to the warehouse and opened up. I turned on the new computer and switched on all the lights. Everything was pretty much set up. I heard the roar of the bikes as they rode into the parking lot. The three Outlaw Souls, a formidable force, stepped off their bikes. All three were dressed in Outlaw vests. Ryder, with his rangy stride, stepped forward first, taking off his leather gloves. Yoda followed, shorter in stature with a few wisps of hair that wafted in the wind – he really needed to stop hanging on to them and cut them off. He had a fat round face that resembled his brother Padre. Trainer was a sight to behold. He wore a sleeveless cut-off shirt that showed off his strong arms with intricate tattoos and ripped abs.

"Hey, the cavalry just came to town." I stood with my hand up in the garage door as they came toward me.

Ryder approached for a hug. "Long time no see, Diego." He looked around and stalked around the place. "Looks good, Diego, real good."

Yoda and Trainer surveyed the high ceilings and the expanse of the garage. "This has a lot of potential. We can really get a large chapter going on here."

I nodded. "It's a great spot. I got a few guys interested, I'm working on their bikes right now."

Ryder walked over to them and looked them over. "Huh. Not bad. We got ourselves a rider. A Harley is a lot of upkeep. He must be serious."

"Looks like it. Do we want to sit and talk about running an open day up here?" I suggested.

"Great idea. I can round up the chapter at the quarterly meeting and we can talk about it. Set a date," Trainer replied.

Ryder placed a heavy hand on my shoulder, lowering his voice. "So let's talk about what's really going on up here. How are the women? Have you bagged any?" The guys laughed.

"Take a seat, fellas. I got coffee here but that's about it. In answer to your question, I met someone pretty special. Unexpected, you know."

Ryder sat at the main table in the office and leaned forward. "Well, let's order pizza and drinks, then we can really get down to business." He paused and looked at me. "Okay, so tell me about her...heritage?"

I stroked my chin and grabbed a notepad and pen. "She's Puerto Rican, she's bad. I'm telling you. Studying to be a doctor. We're working on it, kind of turned cool...but that's Spanish women for you."

Ryder clicked his neck in place. "Ah, a Puerto Rican, she loco?" he laughed.

"Don't you know it. But we Argentinians wouldn't have it any other way." I winked.

Trainer was on the phone calling in the pizza while Yoda waited patiently for us to start.

"What's her name?" Ryder enquired.

"Misty Narvaez."

Ryder and Trainer looked at one another with raised eyebrows.

"What?" I said, puzzled.

"That name sounds mighty familiar..."

MISTY

"You have a maximum of ninety minutes to complete your test. No talking and no eating. If you are caught cheating, you will be escorted from the room and your grade disqualified. This is a multiple-choice questionnaire response for the first thirty minutes of the test. The second thirty minutes will be a case scenario and the third component will be a patient diagnosis where you will be asked to step into the clinical rooms to the left of the hallway. Good luck. Your time starts now."

My palms were sweating bullets. I'd worked so hard that I thought my head would explode from study overload. Words jumped out of my anatomy book and swirled in my brain. I was seated in a large classroom with approximately sixty other students at the University of California. The examiners were standing at the front of the room like soldiers, a large clock ticking away in the background. All the desks were three feet apart. I sharpened my pencil and stared blankly at the circles in front of me. So it came down to this, the first quarter of medical exams in ninety minutes. The sound of the tick from the clock was equal to the pounding in my head. I talked the first question through to myself.

"What would I do if..." First question down, and then it got easier. The information I'd learned started to make sense. My heartbeat eased as I got into the groove of answering the questions. A flash of Shauna and me in the library broke through.

"No, c'mon. Go back to it, that's not right. The pulmonary valve doesn't function if you do that. Read it again." Shauna was a hard taskmaster. She wanted to be a surgeon. That was why she was the best person to study with, and those sessions rang steady and true in my ears. I breathed a sigh of relief as I got through the first thirty minutes of the test. I shook the cramps out of my fingers and looked up briefly. Mostly everyone had their heads down and pencils poised for the remaining questions. Only a few meerkats were peeking around the room. Shauna's curls caught the light at the front of the desks; she too had her head down.

The second part of the test was my forte, and I felt the pencil write automatically under my fingertips. A memory of me as a little girl at my grandfather's house popped up. We'd taken a family vacay to Puerto Rico, and he had me on his knee.

"I wanna be a doctor, Grandpa. I want to help people!" I smiled at the memory. I had pigtails then so I guessed I was around eight years old. I loved it there. My grandfather's house was more like a shack facing the tumultuous Caribbean Sea. The winds would be so strong the palm trees would bend back and forth, howling in the night. The thatched roof would shift and I thought we would get swept away. In all of his forty years living there, he never once was touched by any natural disasters.

"Baby girl, you can save the world. You can be anything you want to be."

I sailed through the questions and headed to the front to drop off my paper. The next part of the test was the doctor-

DIEGO

patient test. I stepped into the examination room where a mock patient sat. I looked at the diagnosis on the clipboard. *Pulmonary heart failure.* I secretly smiled at the one area I'd studied extensively. I breezed through it and blew out a sigh of relief when it was all over. I finished and walked out into the open air. I rubbed my neck, which was sore from holding it in the same position.

Shauna came out looking drained.

"I failed, I know I did. I got the worst doctor-patient scenario. I stumbled over my words and everything!"

I hugged her. "Girl, I know there's no way in hell that you failed. Because if you failed then I'm in trouble. You drilled me and Celine for hours in the library!"

She pouted. "Yeah, I know. I just felt like I didn't do well."

Other students slowly made their way out of the large hall and we walked out to the grassed area to sit down.

"You know what we need?" I said enthusiastically.

She was still in pout mode. "What do we need?"

"We need a beer and wings. Let's go eat and complain about the test. The silver lining is we don't have any more tests today." I smiled. "It's over and it's out of our hands now. In another quarter we'll have another one."

Shauna dragged her feet as we meandered to the car. "Ugh. Don't remind me."

"Let's go to Rondo's. I'm pretty sure it's hot chili wings and beer specials over there."

Shauna perked up. "Oh yeah!"

We drove to Rondo's and parked. Rondo's was this popular bar that had a very cool beer garden out the back. I recognized a few students from the college who were having drinks at the front and chit-chatting. The light airy atmosphere in the space lifted my already happy spirits.

"Hey, my treat, girl. We should have invited Celine! I think she was still in the room after us," I mentioned.

"I know we should have, huh? Oh well, we'll see her in prac in the next couple of days," Shauna dismissed.

"That's true." I nodded my head in agreement.

"Go pick a seat, girl, and I'll bring the beers back," she said bossily.

I leaned over Shauna's back. "Oooo oo. Make sure you get extra ranch sauce!"

She giggled. "Of course, girl."

I retired to the wooden outdoor setting at the back of the bar. I only spotted a couple in the corner canoodling and that was it. The back was littered with palm trees and green plants. As soon as I sat down, guilt set in about not contacting Diego. I sent a quick text through.

"Hey how are you? I miss you and sorry didn't speak. finished exams today xxx"

I looked longingly at my phone, waiting for the text to come through. Shauna with her bright white teeth bounced in with full beers in her hands.

"One for you, my friend, and one for me. Wings coming up!"

She sat the beer down in front of me and when I raised my glass, she chinked hers with mine. "To passing exams with flying colors!" I exclaimed.

"Yes, amen!" I took my first sip and sighed. I stroked the bottom of the glass and looked at Shauna.

"What is it now? I know that look," she said.

"I think I might have been too harsh about a situation."

She smiled. "*Go on*. I think I know what you're talking about," she chided.

"Diego. I miss him. I sent him a text and he hasn't gotten back to me. Maybe I messed up. I just didn't want to be dating some gang-banging biker. My ex was into that shit," I lamented.

"Ahh, baggage." Shauna circled her finger in the air.

I opened my eyes incredulously. "No. It just looks like the same thing."

Shauna sighed. "Or it might not be. Give him a chance and see what it will be. To me, he sounds super sweet. I mean, what guy does a candlelight dinner on a date these days? You'll be lucky if you get a message in your DMs these days. Count your blessings when you have them."

I burst out laughing. "You are so right. The dating game sucks these days." I let the buzz from the beer put me in an even better mood and my phone pinged. My stomach flip-flopped. *Could it be him?*

"Hey babe nice to hear from you. I'm glad about your exams we should celebrate. When you free?"

I did a little squeal in my seat and waved my head from side to side.

"It's him! He wants to celebrate exams with me."

"See, what I tell you?"

"He's saaa sexy," I gushed.

Shauna held up her hand and turned her head in a dramatic fashion. "I don't wanna know. That's enough from lovesick people. Between you and Celine, I'm out."

"Huh? Celine?"

"Yess, honey. Where have you been? Celine and Rob. That night when those creeps came for you. They got together then."

"Ohhh. Wow. That's a nice match. Two doctors-to-be, they'll be fighting over the scrubs."

We laughed at that and our wings came out, piping hot. We dug in and talked some more. By the time we left the bar, the sky had turned a magnificent hue of apricot, that Cali sunset that everyone raved about flooding the skyline. I drove home feeling great about my life.

I walked in the door, "Hey Palo! you in here?"

"Yes, I am." I nearly jumped out of my skin. Palo stood behind me, fixing something on the door.

"What are you doing?"

"I'm checking the alarm pad, that's all. How'd your exams go?"

I replied with hesitation. "They went well. I feel like I did good." He drove the screwdriver through a pad behind the door panel. "Why are you fixing that, Palo?" I asked.

"No reason." His eyes darted around and he wouldn't look me in the eye.

"Palo. I know when you lie to me. Are you beefing up security for some reason? Tell me!" I demanded.

He sighed. "I'm not lying to you. I'm taking precautions. You wanna ride out with me tomorrow? You haven't ridden for a while now."

"You're changing the subject, but that sounds like a plan."

I floated on a cloud back to my bedroom. *Diego texted me back.* Maybe the past was the past like Shauna said. I flicked on the TV in my room and watched a movie to relax. I texted Diego back.

"How about tomorrow night? :)"

"Sounds good babe. Miss you."

":)"

My dreams that night took me to fantasy land with Diego. The memory of his hands cupping my breasts made me toss and turn in my sleep. His lips plundering into me, the aching need and the passion between us. I couldn't wait to see him.

―――

I poured my morning juice when I got up the next morning and waited for Palo to come in.

"Morning," he yawned. "Are you ready to ride? I thought we might take the coastline today."

I put my bread in the toaster. "I'd like that. I heard the dolphins are out right now."

"Yeah, the boys were telling me they saw a few the other day."

I grimaced at the mention of Las Balas, changing the subject. "I can't wait to ride."

"Been a minute, huh? I checked it out, everything looks good."

"Thanks bro'." I smiled at him. "My helmet still there?"

"Yep, it is. No spiders in it." I punched him playfully in the arm.

"Hey!" I yelled.

"Well, I mean you ain't riding, what do you expect? Let me hit this coffee and we'll get out on the road early, okay? Let's head out and cruise to Santa Cruz." My brother made the gesture of his smooth wave and I smiled at his goofball antics.

"Yup. Sounds good." Ten minutes later I was strapped up and ready to go on my Honda Shadow Rider. I'd had her custom-sprayed in purple and loved it. I smiled as I ran my fingers over her before I got on. I signaled my brother to lead and flipped my helmet down. The roar of both our bikes combined got my adrenaline pumping.

Boring ride for a little while, until we got out of Merced city limits. It would take us about two and a half hours to get there. The fresh Cali air flowed around me as I followed Palo's lead, slipping and sliding through the cars. We sliced through the back of Los Banos and San Juan Bautista. I admired the change of scenery through every passing suburb. In the blink of an eye we arrived in Santa Cruz. I stretched my legs out as we parked on the strip close to the beach. I looked out from the town with the rugged coastline hugging the edge of the water. I pulled my phone out and snapped a picture.

"Let me get one of you, doctor-to-be," Palo demanded, chipper.

I handed him the phone and he snapped a cheesy photo of me. "Thanks, bro'. Let's go eat."

"I'm starving." We headed to a café restaurant and sat down out front.

I gasped suddenly, I couldn't help it. I saw his bike. Diego was here, in the same restaurant. Nerves struck me as my mind raced about whether to find him and introduce Palo.

"Hey, what's up with you?" Palo asked. I ignored him.

We walked into a nice family restaurant with modern cuisine and outdoor tables out back and window seats out front.

A blond lady with a pencil behind her head approached us. I looked past her, desperately trying to spot Diego.

"Nice to see you guys. It's table service here, so pull up a seat and we'll come to you." The lady greeted us in a laid-back California way.

"Okay, great," Palo said and turned to see me straining to look out back. "Where do you wanna sit? Out back? Is that why you're looking that way?"

Diego's lion mane was what I saw first. He had his back to me. His hair gave him away. I saw the outline of his hand wrapped around a beer. Next to him was a woman touching his arm tenderly and gazing at him.

"No, let's sit out front," I said bitterly.

"Lady, what's up with you? You look like you want to kill someone."

Latino fire raged through my body as I thought about bum-rushing Diego and telling him where to go.

"I just saw someone I know, that's all."

"Oh no, no. There's more to it." Palo circled a hand to my face. "I can see it."

We sat looking out to the street and the coastline. "Drop it, Palo. I don't even know who she is."

"You taking up smoking again? What are you talking about?"

I sighed. I didn't want my brother keeping things from me so I had to abide by the same rules.

"I'm dating someone and they're here with another female. I don't know who it is though."

Palo pounded his fist into an open palm. "Where is he? Point him out."

"Let's just order, Palo. Sit down."

"No, c'mon, show me what he's trying to replace you with. He's loco if he doesn't want to date you!"

Palo walked a couple of steps to the right side and saw the back of Diego's head.

He sat back down and I watched his jaw twitch. He looked me hard in the eye as the salty breeze swept my hair forward.

"There's no way in hell my sister is dating a direct rival from Outlaw Souls! No fucking way, you hear me!" Palo's voice escalated and patrons turned their heads briefly to see where the sound came from. The fire in his eyes danced like a naked flame.

I held his forearm and pulled him into the seat. "Keep your voice down. We're in the restaurant. Didn't you say you have no rivals? The club is supposed to be going legit?" I raised my brow at him.

"It doesn't matter, there's tension there. We got beef with them. You can't be dealing with them right now. El Diablo is dead because of them."

My mouth formed an O. "He's dead because of Outlaw Souls?" The waitress came to the front table, breaking up our conversation.

"You guys ready to order? Can I get you some drinks to start?"

Palo looked like he was about to axle-grind his jaw off. "No, we're just leaving. No offense, this was a nice establishment, until you let Outlaw bikers in here."

The lady stepped back from Palo's tongue-lashing in surprise. I back slapped him with my hand.

"Palo! Let's go now. I'm sorry about him. He didn't mean it." I sent her my pleading eyes.

She put the pencil back behind her head, mumbled, "Okay," then left.

We walked outside. Now I had to deal with an angry brother and a broken heart.

DIEGO

"How about Santa Cruz? You can take me on a ride for old time's sake."

I winced tightly. "Now's not the best time for you to be coming up here. I got a lot going on with opening the chapter and getting set up. Maybe in a couple of weeks, huh?" I was in the warehouse, counting parts for inventory.

"Umm, too late! I'm here. I came up for the weekend." Crystal put on her baby voice that she used when she wanted something.

"So you're here? You just came up to see me?" I clicked through the new parts I wanted for the shop and ordered.

"No. I wanted to come up there to Yosemite Park as well."

I laughed. "Crystal, you're lying. You hate the outdoors. So unless you've become a completely different person, tell me something real."

"I don't know. I just want to talk to you, like I said, and see how you're doing."

"Okay. You're up. I got a day off tomorrow if you wanna go up to Santa Cruz for something different to do. I can show you the coastline a little bit." *No skin off my nose.*

"Okay, I like it."

"All right, Crystal, let me do my thing here and I'll meet you at mine. I'll text you the address." I let Crystal go from the phone call and sat drumming my fingers on the desk. Misty was the woman I really wanted. As soon as my mind went to her, all I saw was that sexy smile of hers.

I guessed she had come around after all; I got the text yesterday. She inspired me and made me want to do better things with my life.

"Hey how are you? I miss you and sorry didn't speak. finished exams today xxx"

I worked on a few orders at the shop and headed out late. Ryder, Trainer and Yoda agreed to organize a community recruiting day from when they were up here.

"I think if we can get good numbers in the next few months, that's going to be a great start for Merced," Ryder had relayed. "We can get the crew together and line up the bikes, maybe even get some of the younger guys in the chapter to do a show in the parking lot back here."

Yoda chimed in, "We need to show that we're about the community. We stand for brotherhood and not violence. It's time for strong rebranding for the chapter. You're a huge part of that, Diego."

I nodded solemnly. "I'm aware. It's why I joined in the first place, and with the not-for-profits the chapters have been able to support, I think we're changing things slowly but surely."

All in all, Outlaw Souls were changing the guard.

The night passed and Crystal showed up to my door. I had an apathetic feeling when I realized it was her.

"Knock knock!" A sing-song voice greeted me from the other side.

"Who is it?" I played along.

"Your fave stripper from back in the day." I grinned and opened the door.

She'd aged a little with a few crows' feet around the eyes. I scanned her quickly. Her body was still banging but her eyes gleamed with happiness. Her blond hair hung around her shoulders, and she was dressed casually in jeans and a tiger print top.

"Aye! Long time no see. You look good, ma'," I said and meant it. I hugged her close. She smelled of a combination of cigarette smoke and lavender.

"Long time no see, Diego." She stepped back and glanced over me. "You look sexy. Still the man."

I smiled with relief. All the attraction I had for Crystal had died when our relationship ended. When I looked at her, my blood pressure didn't rise like it used to. One sight of her back in the day used to make me wanna jump on stage and grind with her.

"Thank you, baby. You wanna hit the road? It's going to take us about two and a half hours to get down there." Crystal had stepped into the apartment with her hands in her back pockets, looking around. I kept the door inched open and ushered her back out the door.

She regarded me with interest. "Don't want me snooping around, huh?"

I grinned under a nervous façade. "Nah, I mean I wouldn't say that. I just want to take you on this ride. We might see some seals out down there."

She pressed her lips together and stared at me for a second. "Okay, let's hit the road. You still got the second helmet for me?"

"For sure. Hang on tight and we can stop off along the way."

I was a lover of women, and I didn't see anything wrong with catching up with my ex for old times' sake. But a gnawing feeling of guilt made me hesitate. Now Misty was in my life.

We strapped up, the California air feeling crisp against my beard.

"You ready?" I grinned.

"Yep, time for some adventure, for old times' sake."

I took it slower with someone on the back of the bike. Crystal's hands were firmly wrapped around me. Not the same feeling as having Misty's hands there. We cruised at a lightweight pace until we got out onto the open road. I picked up the speed as we hit the freeway. We drifted through the back streets, passing vineyards, the California palms, and old white churches. We stopped through the smaller suburbs and uncovered new places together. We admired the undulating brown-speckled ranges of the California hills, until we reached the iconic Santa Cruz. The bike percolated at a low-level growl as we parked in the main strip. I could taste the fresh saltiness of the air and freedom.

I stretched my arms wide as I got off the bike. "This is why I ride. Man, that felt good. Real nice place, Santa Cruz. I remember riding up here with the chapter when we were together."

Crystal tilted her head as she looked at me. "Yep. I remember that. I was stripping doing double shifts and you were riding a lot. Might have been the reason we broke up."

I grabbed Crystal's hand and said, "We are still talking, just sometimes things don't work out. Nothing to dwell on."

She kicked a pebble under her feet as she looked out to sea. "Yeah. If you say so."

I was starting to rethink the whole ride and doubting if I should have extended the olive branch to her.

"Hey, this place across the road looks good. How about we head in there for a bite to eat?" I pointed to a café with an open window. People were super chill, sitting in the window.

"You been here before?" she asked.

"Yep. On that last ride. They got a nice courtyard out back so we can sit out and get a drink."

Crystal came in close and put her arm around my back and the old affectionate familiarity of us slipped me right back to how we were. From my standpoint it was platonic. I didn't know about Crystal's.

I walked in with a motorcycle helmet in hand, leather jacket and white tee. I ran a hand through my tangled hair. A middle-aged lady with blond hair greeted us with a smile.

"Hey, how you doing? Any outdoor tables out back?" I asked.

"Sure do, follow me." We slid into the wooden outdoor seats surrounded by plants. "Can I get you guys any drinks to start?"

Crystal's bubbly voice rang through: "I will have a Mojito and some nachos."

I raised my eyebrows.

"Right in there, okay, let's go. I'm going to get the tap beer. I don't care what it is. And I will have the nachos too." I smiled at the waitress.

"Okay, easy. Coming right up, guys."

I eased back in the seat. "So, Crystal, what's been happening in your life? Tell me."

"Welp. I stopped stripping a year ago. It was wearing out my body and I didn't like being in the club anymore. Diaz turned into a complete fucking nightmare and started skimming some of our tips for the night. One of the girls he was sleeping with found out he was bankrupt and she told us."

"What the fuck? That's crazy. I'm glad you stopped. I know you were getting tired of it."

"I was. I'm in school now for cosmetology. You know I always like to do my nails and stuff." She twinkled her hands at me and showed off her nails; they were multi-colored with fake jewels at the tips.

"They look good. I'm happy for you. You got any clients?"

"I have about ten clients I see regularly. I'm working on it. So far so good. I feel good, you know? I get to work from home and walk Sammy instead of not being there. It's like he doesn't recognize me anymore. My own dog. Can you imagine?"

"Ha! That little... Ah, I'm going to leave you alone. He was super protective of you. I don't miss him chewing up my shoes."

She laughed softly and hit my forearm. "You leave my Sammy alone. He's good peoples."

"I guess the little puffball's all right." Our beers came and we sipped.

"Sooo. You wanna tell me about the chica you're dating?" Crystal asked.

"She's great, a medical student, studying to be a doctor."

I gauged Crystal's reaction; a flicker of disappointment flashed in her pretty eyes. "Okay, is that it?"

"What were you looking for, Crystal? We just started dating. Are you dating right now?"

She shifted uncomfortably in her seat. "No, I know you're dating someone... I thought there might be some hope for us, now that I'm not stripping anymore..." She twisted her blond hair in her hand.

I drew back, giving her a solemn look. "Crystal, I don't want to hurt your feelings...but we're done relationship-wise."

Her eyes watched me as she sipped her beer. "Is that because of your new girl or something else?" Our nachos came out and I scooped up some beans and guacamole.

"No. Nothing to do with her. It was about you and me. We just have to leave the past in the past, Crystal. Don't dwell on it."

"Okay," she said quietly. "Are you exclusive with her?"

Irritation flashed through my eyes. "Crystal, let it go, baby. I'm not the man for you and you know it."

She crunched her nachos. "You're right."

Awkward silence existed between us for a few minutes. An image of Misty popped up. The light hitting her as she walked with me beyond the trees at Yosemite. I longed for her delicate touch.

Crystal and I talked a little more and made a move to look out over the water.

"So, how's the chapter going up here?" she asked. "You think you'll get the numbers?"

"Yep. I think it's going to work out here. We're for the people. Outlaw Souls has a brotherhood code that we want to expand. I'm all for it."

"That's great you have something to believe in. I feel like that about beauty school. I mean, not a brotherhood but women making other women look good."

"I'm glad you're getting your life together, Crystal. Let's head back."

We rode back a slightly different route, so I could give Crystal a different experience. She held on to me a little too tight, but I didn't mind if it was going to give her some comfort at the end of the day.

"Yo, Crystal, I gotta go right now, okay? Nice to see you but, hey, we have to move on in life. Thanks again for coming out to see me."

"Um, okay. You don't wanna, like...fool around for old times' sake?"

I stood inches from my door and took my helmet off.

"No. I'm good."

"Okay. All the best with the chapter," she said frostily. I just gave her a kiss on the cheek and turned.

When I got inside I saw the missed call from Ryder.

"Hey, Diego. Hit me back when you get this." You couldn't miss his raspy tone.

I hit him back. "Hey, Ryder. What's going on?"

"You sitting down? I got a few things to tell you about your lady friend."

"All right... Shoot."

"You might wanna vet your girls a little more. Your girl's brother is Palo Narvaez. The Las Balas president. He just took over from El Diablo. It's a setup. Tell me, Diego, you're not in on anything with her."

MISTY

Round and round like a merry-go-round, my head spun. As Palo and I rode home from Santa Cruz, I thought about what a web I had gotten myself caught in. Palo yanked his helmet off when we reached our driveway. I put my kickstand down and took off my helmet as well.

"I can't believe you're dating this guy! You gave me the hardest time in the world about criminal activity and now you're going to end up with the same type of dude as last time!" he yelled as the veins in his neck came to the surface.

I put up a finger in his face. "Like hell you're talking to me like this! You vouched for your playboy friend! That's the whole reason I'm living here. He didn't tell me about his dealings right away. I didn't know! Give me a fucking break."

"You didn't know? The guy rides a bike should have been your first clue," he shot back sarcastically.

"Don't even, Palo. Has nothing to do with anything. After you had those motherfuckers of yours try to slip me a mickey at the fucking club!" I screamed, slamming my foot to the ground.

Palo put his hands behind his head and looked to the

heavens. He quickly put his hands together and raised them in my face.

"Don't you understand? Their club was responsible for *killing* El Diablo! Now you're dating the guy who's starting the new chapter. Once he finds out about you, he's going to call in the others. That's the problem." Palo was so mad, spit flew from his mouth and his teeth were bared.

"You don't know that. Diego's not like that with me. He's not *that* guy, his chapter is legit. El Diablo was a piece of shit and ran the club into the ground. So what if he's dead! *El cabron!*"

Palo waved me off. "You're setting the stage for another war! I'm trying to clean it up!" Palo gritted his teeth, slamming the front door behind him. Tears rolled down my face as I put a hand to my temple. Not sad tears, but angry tears. I sensed that Diego would never put me in harm's way. I walked in the house, ready to take a hot shower. I looked at my phone first. There were two missed calls from Diego. I wondered how he had time to text me when he was creeping.

I showered and let the water hit me and wash away the confusion. I dried off and stared at all the books in my room. All the dreams I held in my heart. I stared at my phone and it began to look like Darth Vader to me. I sat on my bed with my hands clasped for a long time. Then I just leaped up and returned Diego's call.

"Hullo?"

"You've been avoiding me," he said.

"I haven't, I've just had a lot going on with exams."

"Is it just exams you've had going on?"

I held the phone away from my face, looking at it.

"I could ask you the same thing," I snapped back at him.

He didn't skip a beat. "I'm down here at the warehouse right now, you should come by." His voice held a threatening tone I had never experienced before.

"I don't know that I want to come there right now."

"Huh? You Spanish chicas love to play games. Come over, I want to see you." His voice smoothed out again and I reconsidered. I was already on my feet and sneaking out of my room. I heard the television on and Palo on the phone. I tiptoed out the back and silently opened the back door to sneak out the side gate.

"I'll be there in twenty minutes, send me the address."

"Okay."

I clamped my hands to the wheel as the evening dusk of night settled in the California skies. I had my window rolled down as I drove and the mosquitos were out to eat. I rolled it up quickly. I turned on my brights as I came to a large warehouse out the back of nowhere. It resembled an old aircraft hangar.

Diego stood close to the side door resting against the doorframe. He had a toothpick in his mouth, his muscles more pronounced than the last time I saw him. His honeycomb hair caught in the light as intense attraction drew me to him like a moth to a flame.

"Misty." Just one word and I thought I would melt right then and there.

"Hey, Diego." I suddenly became shy, but not shy enough for me not to approach him. He pulled me close to him, keeping his eyes open and biting my bottom lip. I closed mine.

I spread a hand on his stomach, softly pushing him away from me. Our greeting made me forget I was mad at him. I walked into the warehouse and looked around. A typical repair shop except for all the space. On the back wall was the club motto hanging as a banner. The place smelled of grease and metal. Two bikes were up on platforms to be worked on.

"Wow, you've set up things so quickly." I turned as Diego

managed to grab a few of my fingers and interlace them with his.

"Yes. I did. Are you avoiding me? Come and sit down. Tell me how you're doing."

I looked back at him. The guy ignited the furnace inside of me.

Diego sat in the closest chair and pulled me into his lap. He grabbed my chin lightly and tasted my lips. All the anger subsided, he pacified me somehow. I pulled back again.

"Diego, are you seeing anybody else?"

His eyes darkened with lust as he replied, "The only person I'm seeing is you."

I wriggled free and stood in front of him with my hands on my hips. "Then why did I see you with a blonde in Santa Cruz?"

A look of complete astonishment flashed across Diego's face. "You were in Santa Cruz?"

"Uh-huh. I was. Tell me about her." He seemed way too cool for my liking. Now the anger came back with a vengeance. "So is that how it's going right now?"

Diego stroked his chin. "One minute you're hot and the next you're cold, mamacita. I waited for you, I understood you needed time. Now I know why...but we'll get to that. Second of all, that blonde was my ex. Ain't nothing going on there. Been there, done that. I'm a man of my word." He pointed to the banner behind him. "See that on the wall. It's all about honor and trust."

I looked at him silently and he studied me for a minute. "Well, what was I supposed to think?"

"You jumped the gun. That could have been anyone. You're supposed to trust me. Back to you. Now it's your turn. I'm going to give you an opportunity." Diego's eyes glowered.

"I guess I have something to tell you."

He nodded his head with smugness. "You sure as hell do.

Funny how it didn't come from you. And you have the nerve to question me."

"You know?"

"Of course I know. So your brother is the president of Las Balas. So it seems like we have a predicament... If you told me earlier then I might have been able to prevent what's going to be coming for you."

My hands trembled. Diego was too calm for my liking. "Diego, what are you going to do? I was scared to tell you. I don't want anything to do with what my brother's club is doing. I couldn't care less. That's why I didn't tell you. That's the whole reason I haven't seen you for three weeks! Because you sure as hell didn't tell me you were in a club from the get-go!"

"Same reason you didn't tell me. I wanted to get to know you. At the time I felt like it was none of your business," Diego responded.

"None of my business that you're in a motorcycle gang? Are you kidding?" I pressed.

"You're sneaky and you didn't tell me you're directly related to a dirty motorcycle club. Ours is legit. We had to handle it. I'm not supposed to even be seeing you."

"What the fuck!" I snapped back.

"Look, let's stop fighting. Come here, mama."

"No. You know what, my brother was right. He told me to stay away from you. Have fun with the female that means nothing to you." I delivered the last blow.

"Same thing I got told. Not to date you. You're bad news, so here we are," he said coldly.

"You know what? I should have known." I glared at him, storming back out to go home. I could feel his eyes on my back as I made it to my car.

DIEGO

All of the lights were out inside the warehouse except for one. I was sitting at the desk, staring at the computer, wondering what just happened. *She saw me with Crystal, goddamn.* I shuffled the papers around on my desk. In a fitful moment, I slid them off. I paced the warehouse thinking and thinking some more. *Las Balas. Palo Narvaez, what do I know about this guy?* I sifted through my mind. I'd never heard Ryder mention him before.

I thought about it some more and headed back to the computer. I looked up the chapter, Las Balas. As I scanned through all the pages, each member had an individual profile. Palo was a short dude with a mean mug in the photo. He had his arms crossed. I read what he had to say.

We are a brotherhood and we stand for Unity. We aim to empower men in the chapter as a stand for solidarity. When you join Las Balas, you're joining a family. We welcome you.

I searched the internet for more information on Palo. I was surprised to find an article about him, another picture with him shaking hands with a Latino not-for-profit organization for kids. He didn't have his jacket on though. I looked closer and he had the name of an organization on the top of his shirt and I couldn't make it out.

My fingers itched to call Misty, I wanted to know what she knew. Her body and the way she moved like water on earth. Her lips, everything in my manhood wanted to go to her. The secret code of conduct in our organization was if you broke the rules, your tattoo was burned off and you were kicked out. Our connection would cause a huge divide.

I didn't have to worry about not calling Ryder; he called me.

"Hey Ryder, how you doing?"

"Good here. Did you break it off?"

"I'm not dating her right now, Ryder. It's my life. I'm not reporting to you about the women I'm with. I know that much," I bit back.

"You just received your nomad patches and the first thing you want to do is date someone from our rival camp? I'm questioning your choices, Diego. I don't care who you fuck. It just doesn't need to be associated with our crew." The silence between two alphas ensued.

"Ryder, like I said to you earlier, I had no idea who her brother was. Get off my back about it."

Ryder's raspy breath pierced through the line. "Stop thinking with your dick. This is bringing heat to the organization. If it gets back to Las Balas, then what happens? We have a potential turf war situation. We just handled El Diablo recently. What... now we gotta handle another one? Think about your brothers, Diego. We ain't got no small chapter, we're at the top of the chain. Other crews are coming for us. Understand?"

"I hear you. But did you look into Palo? He looks clean. I don't know enough but he looks clean. His sister is studying to be a doctor. He's not going to put her in jeopardy."

"Sounds nice in theory, Diego. But men do what they have

to do on the surface. He's already living a double life. He works for some computer company during the day."

"So you did look into him," I shot back.

"Of course I looked into him. That's why I'm telling you. Stay away from her if you know what's good for you." Ryder's warning was clear. The phone went dead.

I looked over the warehouse, flicked off all the lights and headed home. I'd planned to get stuck into the bike on the platform, but I couldn't concentrate.

Man, she looked good. On impulse I sent her a text message.

"I hope you got home alright. let's talk. D."

No way in hell I was going to let Outlaw Souls get in the way of what I had going on with Misty. I opened my fridge and picked up a beer. I let the cold brew hit my throat.

My phone went off and I picked it up without looking.

"Yo."

"Hey, Diego." I swallowed down more beer and retracted the phone to look at it. Misty was on the other end of the line. I leaned forward on the kitchen bench, listening. God, I missed her.

"Hey, you. Did you get home all right?"

"I got home fine. Thanks for the message. I didn't come to argue with you. I missed you." She spoke gently.

"I missed you too. You calmed down now?"

"I'm calm. I never wanted anything to do with my brother's club. You gotta believe me. That's why I didn't tell you. I wanted it not to be there. I wanted to pretend that he wasn't part of a chapter."

I let out a tired sigh. "Misty, be honest with me and tell me... Is your brother drug-running through the club? What the hell is going on over there since El Diablo?"

"I don't know who killed him, but I'm glad. I've been so scared for my brother for the last few years. I asked him to leave the chapter. I want him to live a normal life. I begged him. He wouldn't listen to me. Palo wants to change the chapter around. Do work in the community."

The sincerity in her voice couldn't be missed. I laughed. "Funny, Outlaw Souls want the same thing ultimately. They don't want the stigma either. So here we are, right in the middle of a firestorm." I drained the rest of my beer and set it down on the counter.

"I don't know what to do, papi." She sounded scared.

"I don't see what that has to do with us. You and I can keep going," I said, a heavy silence hanging in the air between us.

"How? Palo's watching me now," she whispered.

"Well, you have class, right? You have to go to school. He can't stalk you forever. It's going to be okay, trust me. To me, we're not against one another."

"I can never seem to keep away from you bikers." I laughed to ease the tension. "Diego. This is too crazy."

"Is it? Do you want me? Because I want you. I don't want to fight about it. I can meet you after class," I declared.

"Me too. I want to see you. I wish we didn't have to sneak around to do this, but if that's what it needs to be..." Misty's voice trailed off. "I'm free tomorrow around one. Come pick me up and we can do something together."

"Sure. I'll call you when I get close. Don't worry so much. By the way, you looked sexy as fuck when I saw you tonight."

"Mmm, you too."

I hung up. I had to see her. I couldn't care less what Ryder had to say.

The next morning flowed a little easier. I rode out to the warehouse with three bikes to work on. All from new clientele. Rick and Derek were coming to collect their bikes as well and talk to me about the chapter. As I worked steadily through the morning, Rick walked in with Derek. I saw them approaching; the warehouse roller door was wide open.

"Hi, Rick, nice to see you again. I got everything lined up for you. Took a minute for that part to come in, that's all."

Rick shook my hand enthusiastically and walked over to the bike. "She looks good. Mind if I test out that hard start in the parking lot? I want to see the difference."

I waved the grease rag out to the parking lot. "Go for it. Please do."

Derek and I watched Rick start his Harley engine and take off. No more crunching, the issue had been resolved.

"How's business going? I see you have a few bikes in here right now," Derek asked as Rick rode.

"Yep. A few of them were referred to me by the chapter. So I'm off to a pretty decent start. I'm keeping my head above water so far." I grinned.

"Good, good. So how many people are you looking to sign up for the chapter?"

"If we get twenty, that will be good."

"Okay, relatively small."

I shifted my gaze to the front of the warehouse as Rick came in from testing out the bike. Two guys in black were standing at the front. One of them was on the slimmer side and poking his head around the edge of the building.

"You've got her running real smooth," Rick told me with an impressed face.

"Yes, nothing wrong with your bike at all, it's in pretty decent condition," I replied, distracted by the two men I'd just witnessed. "Excuse me for a minute, fellas. There's a couple of guys at the front and I need to check them out."

"Okay, no problem," Derek said.

I picked up pace. One fat guy in black and the other guy

looked like a weasel. Both of them looked to be of Hispanic descent. As I got closer, our eyes locked and they backed off.

"Hey!" I yelled out. Neither of them responded; they just kept moving on. I sped up and so did they. I called out again.

"Hey!"

I darted my eyes around the warehouse to see if anyone else was there. They hadn't parked in the parking lot either. Both of them ran to the front of the parking lot and I gave chase. I saw them jump in a black Jeep and screech away from the curb. My breathing picked up from running to catch up with them. *Who the fuck was that?*

Rick and Derek were at the front of the warehouse when I got back.

"Who were those guys? Did you get the plates?" Rick asked.

"Naw. I didn't. I hope that's the first and last time they come around here."

"Where can I sign up for the chapter?" Rick's face was stern. "I'm a bouncer on weekends and it looks like you could use a little help here. You're wide open right now."

"My man." I shook his hand and smiled. "I sure could. We have to initiate you first and the tattoo is part of the code."

"Understood. My cousin told me a lot about you guys already, so I'm across it. You seem like a stand-up guy."

Derek watched and listened. "I'm not so sure. I have a corporate job, so it might not work if somebody finds out."

"No problem, Derek. If you keep coming here to get your bike fixed, that will be fine by me. Rick, I'll call you and we can line up a meeting with Ryder to talk to you. See when we can get you in."

"Okay. Make sure you get the plates on those guys next time. You got my number if you need to hire me for any reason."

"Thanks for the back-up," I said.

"You got a weapon?" he inquired.

"I try not to strap up unless I have to but because of some situations I got a Smith and Wesson."

"You might want to start thinking about bringing it."

"I hear you. Glad that didn't deter you from wanting to join."

"Nope."

"Okay, I'll be in touch."

As Rick and Derek made an exit, I rifled through my head as to who might want to start trouble. If I told Ryder about it, he would probably connect it to Las Balas. I looked down at my watch. I was due to pick up Misty in the next hour so maybe she would know something about it.

Time flowed on and I hit the road on my bike to see Misty. I parked my bike in the medical school parking lot and waited. I got a few stares, mainly at the bike. I gave them all a customary salute as they whispered amongst their friends.

Suddenly I felt the back of my bike start shaking. I snapped my head around quickly.

"Ayy!" Behind the voice was a beautiful Puerto Rican lady, Misty.

"You lucky. I was about to start something." I grinned as she closed the gap and came to me.

I wrapped my hands around her hips easily as she leaned in for a kiss.

"Mwah! I was just playing. You looked bored so I wanted to shake you up a little."

"Good job," I whispered. "How was class, where are your friends at? I wanted to meet them."

"Just me today, next time you pick me up you can meet Shauna. I don't have the same classes as everyone else today."

"Okay. Are you ready to go? How about we grab a bite to eat?"

"Sounds good. You gotta drop me back here in a few

hours though. I have a late class."

I squeezed her hand as she talked, her radiant Spanish beauty taking me over. "I can do that for you."

We rode out to a nice café around the back of Merced. Eyes were out; Ryder had connects in Merced, so we kept it low-key. We got a table at the back of the café, and I looked around as we walked through. The place looked like a ghost town. The sign on the counter said table service so we headed to a booth at the back. Spanish music ran through the speakers.

"Hmm, I don't think anybody is going to find us here."

I smiled at Misty. "I know it's a little out of the way, but I don't want to take any chances. There's a lot at stake. But I had to see you. I miss you in my bed and in my arms."

"You are so sweet. Can I get a kiss?" she asked sexily. We were sitting side by side, and she linked her leg across mine as I grabbed her face. I let my lips drift over hers, her soft juicy lips breathing life into mine.

"Mmm. You taste good. Stop, otherwise we'll need to go to your place." She lowered her voice seductively.

"Fine by me, just say when, baby." Her sexy legs were wrapped in black jeans and she wore a cute red top that matched her temperament.

A slight young boy with dark hair, no more than fifteen, came to the table. He looked to be of Spanish descent.

"Ola, can I take your order today?"

"Yes, can I have a latte and one of your enchiladas?" asked Misty.

"Little man, can you add another latte to that and two chili tacos?"

"Si. Be right back." As the little boy walked away, I focused on Misty.

"I want to talk to you about something," I said. Her feline olive eyes held their own, and I wanted to bite her lip. "Do you know anyone from Las Balas that might start a war? I am asking because I had an incident at the warehouse this morning." Her eyes remained steady but her body tightened up. I put my hand across her thigh, rubbing it. "I'm just asking you. Don't fly off the handle like last time."

"It's not that. I don't want anything to happen to you. I didn't tell you about something because I didn't want you to worry."

I looked her square in the eye. "Misty! This shit ain't for play play. You need to tell me what you know. All of it. *Now!* I can't protect you if you don't tell me." The darker side of my Argentinian passion came out.

She licked her tongue around her lips as her eyes taunted me. "Oooh, I like it when you get angry, papi. Fierce." She flicked her long hair out of her face. I waited patiently for her to answer. "I was at the club, The Partition and these two guys in all black from Las Balas came in. They bum-rushed me at the bar and asked if I like to fuck. My bro' came and picked me up. I was shaken up a little. He told me he kicked them out of the chapter though."

Our coffees came out with our meals. The little guy had them on a platter.

"Thank you for your order. Here you go."

"Thank you." We both said in unison.

"What the fuck? You should have called me. I would have come got you," I hissed.

"We'd only just started dating then. I didn't really know you like that," she replied as she picked at her food.

"Still. So what do these guys look like?" I bit into my taco and the sauce squeezed out the side.

"One was really slim but slimy, wearing all black, the other one was fat and wearing black too. He had this teardrop between his fingers."

"Teardrop between his fingers," I repeated as my mind

started racing. "Let me find out about that. Fits the description of the two guys I saw. Misty. You gotta tell me what's up. Don't leave me hanging in the dark about what's going on."

"I know now. I promise I won't." We ate in silence and in the back of my mind I wondered if this was a set-up. I shook it off. "You mad?" she enquired as she finished her meal.

I sighed and touched her forearm lightly. "Baby, no. I just don't want any bullshit. I didn't come here for this."

She lowered her head and looked into her food. "I'm not trying to bring trouble to you. I had no idea about these guys, I swear."

"I believe you. Let's just chill with it." I crunched the last of my tacos. They went down easy. We sat eating quietly and we exited not long after. The ride was relatively silent as we both got lost in our own thoughts. I dropped her back at the university.

"Misty, be careful and call me if anything else like that happens."

"I will." She raised her hands around my neck and massaged my head. I loved her touch and could stay holding her forever. I knew I had to let her go, though. I tapped her lightly on the ass.

"Go, go. Get to class before we never make it out of the parking lot." She giggled and gave me a quick kiss.

The next few days went by and the disturbing feeling about those two guys kept me up at night. I researched the Las Balas page, looking for the two members and new clues. I couldn't see them on the page. Maybe Misty was telling me the truth after all.

I'd gotten into the routine of heading to the warehouse early around seven a.m. I tied up my dirty blond hair and wore the same blue denims as always and a white tee. I opened up when I got there and flicked on all the lights. I'd started with three bikes for the week and now there were two left. Both of them were Honda touring bikes. Nothing out of the ordinary, just standard services. I boiled some water to make an instant coffee and turned the radio on.

The sounds of pistons rang through the warehouse and I perked up at the thought of more business. Some sound off in the distance caught my attention. The water jug boiled and I poured my instant coffee. I stepped to the front of the warehouse which led onto the street. I looked out and in the quickest of flashes, noted a guy on a bike parked yards away. Just watching. Again in all black. When I stepped out to look closer, the bike sped off.

The shitstorm was officially beginning. I sipped my coffee and ran my mind back to where I'd hid my gun. The last time I had to use it was on a rival gang back in the day.

"*Get the fuck off my property before I call the crew!* We don't have your drugs, now fuck off!" I shook my head. I'd just gotten home from a ride out with the boys and they were having some trouble with the Notorious Riot gang. I had been warned that I would need to carry.

Kicking and loud banging thundered through my ears so hard and fast I thought I was dreaming. My adrenaline shot through the roof and on beat I reached into my bedside drawer and clicked my clips in place, ready to quick draw. Two masked men of average height were in my La Playa kitchen, sniffing around that night. Too busy searching for shit they didn't see me in the white wife-beater and cut-off shorts aiming a Smith and Wesson at their heads.

"Looking for something, boys?"

"Oh shit!" one of them hollered. They clocked at breakneck speed to get out of the screen door. I shot at the ground to make them dance a little. That sped up their pace considerably.

Another reason to leave La Playa... Too many memories from the early days.

MISTY

Running my hands through Diego's rough stubble made me want to ride off into the sunset with him, just like in the old cowboy classics. My daydream was burst by a late biomedical class where we were examining cultures and blood types in the lab.

"Hey, hot stuff. What's cracking with you?" Shauna with her bouncy jet black curls and fresh lip gloss was lined up behind a microscope. We were in the clinical labs with a handful of other students.

"Oh, plenty." The whites of her eyes became more prominent as she scanned me dramatically.

"You were with the biker hottie, weren't you? Why haven't I met him?"

"Oh, you will in time. He asked the same thing about you. He wants to see you. I told him next time you can meet." The dreamy smile couldn't be wiped off my face, and I felt like I could just drift on out of the classroom. Mrs. Sanderson, a redheaded middle-aged woman with curly hair said:

"You'll notice you each have two slides in front of you. I simply want you to describe what you see and tell the class.

One is blood plasma and the other is bacteria. Your turn." She flipped over a whiteboard and the squeak of her blue marker filled the room. I squinted my eye through the microscopic lenses in front of me and drew back. I was looking at the bacteria. An orange ring of intricate circles joined together and a mustard yellow ring on the inside with a purple blob in the middle. Some were a sickly shade of green. When you looked at the liquid on the glass itself, it just looked like a blob.

"Check that out. It's amazing," I said, pointing.

"Lemme see. Lemme see." I stepped aside and let Shauna take a peek. "That's crazy. I don't know what it is but I hope I never get it," she said loudly.

Mrs. Sanderson laughed, along with a couple of others in the class.

"I mean, am I wrong, guys, come on, right?" She shrugged her shoulders and made a face like the Cookie Monster from Sesame Street.

"You're not wrong. Funny you should mention you hope you never catch it...because what you're looking at is influenza."

The whole class gasped, including me.

No way!

That's crazy!

Ewww.

The class ended up being a really interesting two hours and we received an assignment on identifying clusters and different types of blood plasmas for our trouble.

"I'm glad to get out of that lab. I always feel like I'm trapped when I'm in there," I said.

Class was done for the day and I was heading home. Huge puffy clouds crossed the Cali sky and it looked as if she was about to unleash her tears on us.

DIEGO

"Girl, I'm not trying to get wet. I'm about to run to the car right now. You need a ride home right?"

"Yup. I do," I said hesitantly. Shauna took off her jacket and put it over our heads like a blanket as we skittered off. I loved listening to the patter of rain falling. Students ran past us. Looked like they forgot their umbrellas too. I wasn't in a hurry to get back home, but it was inevitable. I had a real estate pamphlet in my bag that I'd picked up. I planned to make good on the promise I'd made to myself. I wanted to move out of the house. I was starting to feel stifled.

A break in the weather and a peek-a-boo from the sun let me know it was just a passing Cali shower. Shauna and I walked with her to her car. Mainly, I was dreading getting home to an onslaught from Palo. He'd been looking at me strangely ever since the Santa Cruz ride. Shauna and I were both silent most of the way. We'd talked enough in class. She dropped me right at my door.

"Okay, girl. I'll see you tomorrow," she said giving me a quick hug.

"Thanks Shauna. Don't study too hard," I told her with a smile.

"I won't. I'm taking a break. My brain's fried," she replied in a tired voice.

I walked in the door and headed to the kitchen. I could hear Palo talking in the den. The door was cracked and I saw a shadow of his bald head. He was tapping something on the desk.

"What did you do? Are they gone now?" Palo asked in an exasperated tone. I flattened myself against the wall so I could hear what he was saying and who he was talking to. "You don't know what happened to them? I told you to scare them enough to get rid of them. Now we got a situation, right? I can't take the chapter forward if we have this situation." The daggers of anger were sharply directed to the person at the other end of the line. "I got to go check out this Diego guy." I felt my chest rise and fall from anxiety. Why the hell was he talking about Diego? "He needs a warning. I'm about to go find out. I know my sister, she gave up too quickly. She'll find a way to see him."

I wrinkled up my nose in disgust. Another vote for leaving my brother's house. I didn't want him tracking my whereabouts. I tiptoed on the balls of my feet to the kitchen and picked out some cheese and crackers from the pantry. A red wine was sitting on the counter and I poured myself a glass. It would help while I studied bacterias. I made myself the plate and headed to my room. I wanted to warn Diego about my brother. If he wanted something, he would be ruthless enough to go after it. I texted him as soon as I sat my evening snack down on my desk.

"Heads up my brother might pop up to talk to you. I overheard."

The phone vibrated with a blue screen, Diego was calling me.

"Hey, what the hell?" His exasperated tone made me nervous. "I thought he didn't know about us?"

"He doesn't, he's going based off when I saw you in Santa Cruz."

"Tell me again he has nothing to do with those fucking peasants from his club. If this is a set-up it ain't a good idea. Outlaw Souls will stitch this up real quick so you need to tell me now. It will turn into a full-blown turf war and there's no turning back from that. Bloodshed will be what's up next on the menu."

I sighed, taking a sip of my wine to calm my nerves. "Diego, stop thinking like that. It's not a set-up. My brother wants to talk to you because he is overbearing. He's protective. He wants to talk to you because you're dating me."

Diego paused for a minute. "So you have two men standing over you."

"It's not like that, Diego."

"I know. I'm just frustrated. I want to be with you, out in the open. I want to spend time with you and not have this bullshit hanging over our heads."

The back and forth of hiding and sneaking was starting to grate at me as well. "How do you think I feel? I have classes, I'm trying to become a doctor and I'm dating an Outlaw! You see why I didn't want to talk to you?"

He laughed. "Dating an outlaw? Not quite, baby doll. But hey, sounds badass doesn't it?"

"It does. Hang on a minute." I crept to the door and opened it. Nobody was there. I wanted to check that Palo wasn't listening in on my conversation. Then I heard the sound of high-speed cars and knew he was playing a video game in the main lounge.

"What happened?"

"Umm. I was checking for Palo. He's playing video games, the coast is clear."

"Okay. I know you gotta study but I will be ready. Has your brother got a cool head? Is he coming at me with a few people or not? Let me know now so I know what I'm up against."

"Papi! He's not coming at you that way. He will approach you man to man. That's not his style. He's old school. I wanna say something else..."

"What now, Misty? Please, between the two punks that tried to bum-rush my warehouse and your brother, what else could there be?"

"I don't know. Misunderstanding between you and me about that friend of yours. Crystal was it? He was mad because I was crying about it."

"You really thought I was with her? Oh, man."

I cringed a little. "See, that's why I didn't want to tell

you," I said as I grabbed a piece of cheese and put it on a cracker.

"Crystal and I ran our course. She came to see me to close the door I guess."

A pang of jealousy hit me. "I guess I can't compete with that."

"There's nothing to compete with. I want you and *only* you. I wouldn't be jumping through all the hoops I am right now. We just need to tread lightly. I'll go easy on your brother when he gets here. I won't rough him up too bad." Diego laughed wholeheartedly on the other end.

"Stop!" I responded playfully.

"It will work out," he said simply.

"Okay. I trust you."

"That means a lot. I know you gotta study, so I will let you study to save the world. You wanna come here later in the week?"

"Yes, if I can swing it."

"We'll figure it out. Bye, baby."

"Bye."

I planned to put a stop to the situation. I just had to broach the subject from a different angle with my brother. I had a day off the next day. Well, not technically, just a lecture I didn't feel like going to. I wanted to give myself a break from things and to talk to Palo. We met like we always did in the kitchen for breakfast. He looked bleary-eyed as he got ready to head out the door for his day job. I had a coffee in my hand. I turned to face him.

"Morning, Palo." I was still in my PJs and he hadn't even seen me.

"You're still here? I thought you would be at school."

"No. I have a day off." I sipped some of my coffee and continued, "I know you're going to speak to Diego."

Palo froze and glanced over at me. "How do you know that?" He blindly reached for the coffee pot.

"I heard you. Don't do it, Palo. He's not doing anything sinister. I told you that. You're literally trying to ruin things for me."

Palo poured his coffee into the cup. "This has nothing to do with that. Besides, if you're dating the guy, I'm going to need to see him at some stage. He has a new chapter operation. I need to check the temperature. If he's feeling a certain kind of way then we may need to rectify that. Plus the guy had you in tears."

"Stay out of it, Palo. It wasn't what I thought it was." I opened the refrigerator, looking for the juice.

"I could say the same to you. This is about the chapter. You didn't want to be involved, remember? Why couldn't you just date someone in your league? Like a med school student or a normal guy that works a day job from the suburbs or something?" He flipped his hand up at me.

"Do I tell you to stop dating strippers? How about that? Don't you work for a computer company? Please, Palo. Save me the judgment from you of all people." I turned and walked back to my room, slamming the door. I fell back on my bed and stared at the ceiling. *How did I get to this place?* Once Palo made up his mind to do something, then that was what he did. My brother might have appeared calm, but that didn't mean anything with him.

DIEGO

Two weeks passed and the men in black hanging around the front of the warehouse were nowhere to be seen. Still left me triple-checking the warehouse locks and resetting the alarm code several times.

It was mid-morning in the office and my legs were up on the counter. I had the phone in my hand talking to Ryder.

"Hey, Ryder, you good down there?"

Ryder's barreling tone came through the line like a freight train. "Diego. We are good down here. Business as usual. What about you at that end? You moved on from that Las Balas situation, right?"

"You've got nothing to worry about. Things are running right here." I broke out into a sweat on the back of my neck. I rubbed it with my free hand to ease the tension. "Listen, I called because we have two new potential members. Derek and Rick."

"Oh yeah? Tell me about them, what's their MO?"

"Rick mainly, Derek seems a little shaky, but I think he might join up once Rick does. Not that I'm trying to rush the numbers. We want quality over quantity, right?"

"Right. Keep going."

"Rick would be handy to us. He has a background in security."

Ryder grunted. "Huh. We could use him. Give him my number and let me talk to him. Set something up. You got another vest up there?"

"Yeah. I think I do."

"Has it got all the patches on it already or we gotta sew them on?"

"Nope. All the patches are already on it."

"Okay. Keep an eye out for this Palo guy. I want you to be vigilant up there. Let us know how we can help you, all right?"

"Done deal."

"Oh, and Diego. Don't think we won't hesitate to hit Las Balas if we think we need to."

"I know." I set the phone down and ran a hand through my hair. There were a few tangles at the bottom so I pulled them out. I slammed my fist on the table out of frustration. I was kicking myself for telling Ryder about Misty at all.

I flashed my old life through my eyes, sleeping with a gun on my bedside table and Crystal coming home from the strip club at two in the morning smelling like the whole liquor cabinet.

"Why you gotta drink so much?" I'd ask. She would stumble and her hair would be a complete mess. Her legs would cross and she would trip over her own feet while clutching the bedsheets to stop her from falling.

"Oh, you don't love me anymore, do you?" she would slur and start to cry.

I would lie to her. "Yes, I do. I just wish you would stop killing yourself with the drinking. If you don't like the strip club, stop working there."

"Shuddup. You don't pay my bills. You don't know what it's like!"

I closed my eyes, shaking off the memory. She looked a lot different when I'd seen her. She'd cleaned up a lot. I was proud of her.

That life was not something I wanted a repeat of here in Merced. I got up to stretch my legs and peruse the parking lot. I walked back and forth, checking the perimeter. I peeped out on the street just for good measure. Nothing. This part of the street had barely any businesses around it. It was me and two other warehouses tucked away in an avenue. Good for biker association business, but not necessarily for motorcycle repairs. I strolled back and thought about why those bozos would have wanted to case out the warehouse. My mind drifted back to what Misty said about them propositioning her. Seemed like the move of a pimp. Especially with two of them flanking her either side of a bar. The two-for-one special. My blood ran hot thinking about what I would do if Misty was harmed.

I checked the ground, looking for clues. There were none, just smooth asphalt. I sighed as I entered the warehouse and suited up with my coveralls, ready to get down to the business of bikes. I had new parts coming in for one of the two bikes I had left to work on. Turned out one of the Hondas needed more than just a service. It had a little vibration issue going on. Nothing worse than having a bike with a jarring motion underneath you. I test-ran it in the parking lot and knew then I couldn't give it back without fixing that issue.

I walked to the back of the warehouse and picked up my cell phone, making the call. I paced the warehouse while I did. I didn't feel like sitting down.

"Hi, I want to ring in for compression and rebound adjusters. Have you got any in stock?"

"Uhh, lemme check. Just hold the line for a minute."

"Okay, no problem." The lady on the line came back a few minutes later.

"Yep, we have them in stock. Were you looking to place an order?"

"Yes, I want to place an order. I think I already have an account with you. It's under Diego Christopher."

"Let's see here. I'm just checking my computer... Diego... Okay. Yep. Here we go. I see it. No problem. We'll add these parts to the account and bill you at the end of the month."

"Okay, great."

"Is there anything else I can do for you today?"

"Yeah, how long will that take to come in?"

"We can get it to you this afternoon. When do you need it?"

"This afternoon would be great."

"Anything else, sir?"

"No. That's it. Thank you."

I hung up. Another one down.

I rang Rick next.

"Hey, Rick, how are you, man?" I kicked some annoying piece of dust up from the ground as I noted the grime on the warehouse windows. I needed to get that cleaned asap.

"Hey, Diego! Nice to hear from you, man. Any news?"

"Yeah, I have some. I wanted to connect you to the club president, Ryder. He wants to talk to you. You know, just to get to know you and see where your head is at. I told him about your security background and that's a real bonus for us."

"For sure, pass my number through to him and we can talk. I got a few guys that can, you know, step in if times get rough. You get a look at those two goons that came past your warehouse?"

I grimaced as I looked down at my unlaced boots. "No. They did another lap, but that was two weeks ago. I haven't seen them since then. I'm keeping an eye out. I have you in mind, so thanks for the back-up."

"Any time. I look forward to the call from Ryder."

"Bike running all right?"

"Incredible. I feel like a new man."

I laughed at the familiarity of what he said. *The freedom that riding brings is addictive to the soul.*

"Thought as much. Listen, give me a call after you speak to Ryder and we'll get that vest for you. Just some formalities to go through with getting you sworn in. But unofficially, welcome to the family of Outlaw Souls."

"Thanks, man. Don't forget what I said though."

"I won't." I hung up the phone. All the phone calls I wanted to make for the day were out of the way, except for one that was most important to me. I had a few other things to do in the warehouse and Misty's voice was the one I wanted to end the night with.

I turned the music up loud and drowned everything out as I scanned the Honda on the platform. I ran an engine check with a compression test and checked out the oil pressure. I topped it up and ran the engine again. I listened to the beautiful hum. Satisfied, I moved to the aesthetics of the bike. The fender had a crack in it. Nothing major. I had the right glue to put a hold in it. I repaired bikes but I didn't do the aesthetics unless it was banging out the lumps and bumps. I'd found a contact who did it in Merced and I thought I would pass it onto the bike owner. I put my hands on the tires and tested them, observing the tread. Not bad, in good condition. Looked like the rider hadn't taken the bike out for a while. Next, I tugged at the cables and checked their inputs and they were in good condition too. Aside from a couple issues, this Honda was an easy service to work with. I made good time and when I looked up at the warehouse clock it was twelve p.m. I worked steadily until four. No excitement jumped off in the warehouse. It was eerily quiet. I flicked off the radio and stepped out of my coveralls. The weather was a little muggy, triggering a memory of riding twenty-deep with my brothers and engines, purring down the highway to Tijuana. I chuckled as I thought about it.

I mounted my bike and headed over to The Partition, the same place Misty had ended up at. Looked different in the light of day, not so glamorous. Not so many cars in the parking lot either. I dismounted from my bike and headed into the bar. A dude with spiky hair came to me.

"Hey, man, how are you doing? What can I get for you?"

"I'll take a Jack and Coke." He winked and doubled back. "You want ice in that?"

"Yes please." I looked around with interest. Weird music. Some trance-like beat. A couple in the back who should have gotten a hotel room and another lady who looked like she'd had some surgery done. She caught my eye and winked. I glanced at her. Her dark auburn hair looked like a weave. Big breasts, definitely enhanced; they didn't move as she walked. She was wearing a green skin-tight dress that stopped at the bottom of her coochie. She had it all hanging out. Big brown eyes and large plump lips. I smiled a little as I found it amusing. I watched as she made her way to me.

"Hey there, Mr. Biker Boy. How you doing?" She ran her finger across the back of my neck and it made goosebumps stand up on my neck. I flicked her off.

"What can I do for you?" I asked in an irritated voice.

"Well, it's the other way round. I wanted to know what I can do for you." She slid in the barstool next to me and perched her face in her hand.

"Not a goddamn thing." The bartender looked at me and then looked at the frisky woman and sat my Jack down in front of me. I picked it up with my thumb and index finger and let the black liquid slide down my throat. I gave her the side-eye.

She laughed with a husky tone and touched my forearm. I drew it back.

"Oh stop it, you're flattering me. It's too much," she giggled. I gave her a flat-out glare. "Look, I gotta make my money somehow. Plus I saw your patches on the back of your vest. I thought you might be up for it. Most of you are up here." She'd piqued my interest now.

"Okay, so you got a few on a roster, do you?"

"Yes, I do, honey. They love them some Mimi."

I laughed then and loosened up. "Mimi, can I buy you a drink? I don't wanna fuck you, though. I got a girl. But I'm sure you get a lot of work." I looked her over once more.

She beamed. "Sure, I wouldn't mind a drink and thanks for not sending me away."

"You're welcome."

I put up one finger to the bartender and whispered to Mimi, "What you drinking?"

"I'm having what you're having..." She licked her lips and ogled me some more. I sat still. The bartender didn't have much to do. He was busy wiping down the bar and headed our way.

"Hey, Mimi, what are you sippin' on?" She pointed to my drink. He saluted her and smiled. "Got it."

"You know him?" I asked. She repositioned herself on the stool.

"Yep. I come here a lot. My customers are here."

"Okay."

"Here you go, Mimi." Mimi took her drink and rocked to the beat in the club.

"So you were talking about bikers. Are a lot of them in here and where are they from?" I waited for her answer patiently.

"Hmm, some retired bikers that aren't in chapters anymore. But I have regular clients from Las Balas."

My ears perked up. "Las Balas, huh? Anyone I know?" I grinned to make her comfortable.

"Hmm. I don't know who you know. But two guys tried to recruit me. They were trying to pimp me. Slapped me around after the fact. I had to run and call my other girls. We got a code. I warn 'em about hitters."

My back bristled. I hated men who hit women. "I'm sorry that happened to you, Mimi. You good now?"

"Yeah, I'm good now." I could tell she wasn't, her big eyes looking into the Jack. She threw back another sip. "Two guys in black. One fat dude and some other weasel. Both of them had small penises. Quick money though. Made my quota for the night. They paid big and had some good drugs."

"Okay, well there's that. So they're trying to recruit your ladies? Your crew."

"Yep." She nodded her head up and down profusely. "They are, but all the girls won't go near them. I warned them all. The streets are talking, know what I mean?"

I saluted Mimi with the last of my drink and threw it back. "I know exactly what you're talking about."

She tilted her head at me and looked closely.

"What is it?"

"You're a real nice guy. Respectful to ladies. I'd fuck you for free."

I laughed so hard. Mimi laughed right along with me.

"Thanks, I take that as a compliment, Mimi. Look, I gotta bounce. Take care of yourself out in the streets."

"Okay, biker boy. What's your name?"

"Diego. Nice to meet you."

"You too. Bye, sweet thang." I smiled at her brazenness. I tipped my hat to the bartender. He waved back. Only one Jack to ease the tension from the uncertainty that swirled around me. Now more information had opened. A pro' ring. I should have known.

MISTY

Secret date night with the hunky and chiseled Diego. I knew I was falling in love and I had all my barriers down for him to walk into my heart. I hoped he didn't break it.

    Palo was out for the night; I checked. I had to creep and listen to his conversations to see when I could make it over there. I kissed the saint behind my desk which was part of our faith as Puerto Ricans. I wore one of my new panty-and-bra sets with a black maxi dress. I sprayed the peachy perfume I had in the air and walked into it, Beyoncé style. I straightened my hair and let it hang. I smoothed a nice clear lip gloss over my lips. If I wore my red lipstick he was just going to lick it off anyway. A smile formed on my lips as I slipped out of my room. I walked to the car and delicately slid in. A delicious excitement about the danger involved in being with Diego was making my blood hot with lust. What we had was like biting into forbidden fruit.

    I made it to Diego's house twenty minutes later and parked beside his badass bike where the chrome shone bright in the moonlight. It was clear out, with stars twinkling bright in the sky. I walked to Diego's apartment complex and knocked on his door with a specific beat.

Diego answered the door with desire plastered all over his face. He had on a wife-beater, a three o'clock shadow and low-slung jeans. As always, his feet were bare. His muscles rippled and made his wife-beater sit just right. His dirty blonde hair was down. There was no talking. He scooped me in through the doorway with one arm in such a snap-second I nearly lost my balance. He looked at me with his hooded blue eyes before taking over my lips, tasting, plundering and discovering. The hot Latin fire burned deep between us. The passion of his kiss made me lose my breath for a moment. I heard a low rumbling groan in his throat and felt his manhood rise. He eventually let go of me and stepped back. I gasped and smiled wide.

"That's how much I missed you," he said, stroking the edge of my jawline.

"Papi. I like it. I will have to stay away from you more often." I gave him sultry eyes.

"Please don't," he pleaded.

"I won't, that won't work for me either," I giggled. He looked at me with the ocean-blue swimming in his eyes as he licked his lips.

"You look beautiful. And you smell damn good. You're trying to give a man a heart attack." He closed his eyes and got two wine glasses down out of the cabinet.

"No, I would never. I like to dress nice when I'm not at school. I figure I'll be in scrubs for the next half of my life, so why not?"

"I like you both ways. You're even more beautiful naked and in my bed."

"Mmm," I cooed.

"Red? I got us an antipasto platter too. Then we can think about what we want to eat."

"You're so thoughtful. It amazes me."

"I keep telling you, baby, people got me fucked up. I'm a lover."

"That you are," I agreed.

"Go take a seat and I'll bring it over."

I sat on the couch and crossed my toned legs, waiting for Diego to come and sit with me.

"Put some music on. You like olives?" he asked with one in his mouth.

"Love them."

"Okay, good." He came around to the coffee table with a selection of cheeses, crackers, olives, sun-dried tomatoes, dip and pastrami.

"This looks good." I popped an olive between my manicured fingers and into my mouth.

Diego's eyes glowed with intensity at me. "I like the way you eat that olive."

I giggled. "Stop it!" He grinned and put his warm hand around my knee, resting his head back on the couch and crossing his knee over the other one.

"So listen, I wanted to talk to you about a few things."

"Okay, baby, go ahead," I said.

"Ryder is still on Las Balas and now I have more information about what's going on. I need you not to lie to me."

I frowned at him. "What do you mean not to lie? I told you I'm not already."

He gripped my knee tighter and looked at me. "Las Balas is trying to start a prostitution ring. Those two guys that were harassing you at the club thought you were one. That's why they were so persistent."

I froze with disbelief at what I thought I was hearing from him. "So? I told you that. My brother doesn't have anything to do with that. He wouldn't be involved; he kicked them out. He promised me."

Diego searched my eyes, giving me a pitiful look. "Just because he told you he did doesn't mean he did. Las Balas has never been known as a clean club. Why would they start now? He was under El Diablo's reign, he would have been a witness to a whole other side. If you're not part of the solution, you're part of the problem."

I gasped in horror. "How the hell are you saying this? I don't even understand."

Diego put another olive in his mouth like nothing was happening. "Well, I've seen and known a lot in my time, ma'. Don't get out of pocket. I'm not saying you're involved. I just don't know about your brother. How do you know for sure? Think objectively."

I took my shoes off slowly. "Don't get out of pocket, is that what you said?" I had a hand under his chin.

"Well, yeah. Just relax a little. I'm only talking." My bare feet were grounded to the floor. An interesting look took place on Diego. I rolled my toes back and forth. I jammed my foot on top of his, just enough for him to yelp a little. "Owww! What the hell, Misty!"

I narrowed my eyes and flicked my hair.

"That's how out of pocket I'll get." The electricity of sexual tension pulsed through my body and Diego fed off it. He grabbed my foot and brought it to his mouth to kiss it.

"Get over here. Is that how we're getting down tonight, huh?" he whispered playfully and slid me over to his lap so I could look in his eyes.

"Don't play with Spanish women, you know we loco," I warned.

He had his hands cupped around my buttocks, caressing them. He admired the flicker of my lioness gaze. I felt his arousal as I grabbed the top of his shirt into a fist.

"And I love it," he gritted through his teeth. I made a V

with my hands and grabbed his jaw. I crushed his lips with mine and he groaned softly.

"Let's forget about dinner. You can be mine."

"I'll agree to that." He smiled darkly.

I leaped off him, expecting to follow him to the bedroom but to my delight, he grabbed me by the waist and put me over his shoulder, smacking me on the buttocks. My long dark hair hung almost down to the ground as he walked us to the bedroom.

As we reached the darkness of his lair, the vibration of his phone ringing sounded through. He let it ring. Diego placed me down on the floor and faced me toward the front of the bed with my back to him. He was behind me and rubbing me up from behind. The phone vibrated on the bedside table again.

His hot breath hit my ear. "Hold on. Let me turn that off." My body was ready to be thrown into the throes of desire. "Shit!"

"What is it?" I felt frustration hit as my sexual desires got redirected.

"The alarm code has gone off at the warehouse. I gotta go over there. You ridin'?"

"Of course. Let's go," I said but it came out reluctantly.

Diego flung open the closet door and pulled out his rustic biker boots, sliding into them easily. He laced them up. His club vest was hanging in the closet and he put it on swiftly. At the bottom of the closet was the second helmet.

"Here."

"No. Diego, let's take my car and go now."

"You sure?"

"Yes. Let's ride." I felt like Bonnie and Clyde riding with my man. I picked up my purse from the kitchen counter as Diego walked ahead of me and yanked the door open. His face was pure concentration. He was ready for battle. I saw something I didn't want to see. That was him strapping up. He put a gun holster on and slid his Smith and Wesson into its slot. *Shit.* "I'll drive," I said.

"Okay. Keep to the speed limit. Whatever they decided to do, it's been done already. Let me call Rick and see if he can back me up out there. If this is who I think it is, we got some heat coming our way." Diego's eyes flashed with anger in the passenger seat. The streets were lit up and people were out. The traffic was reasonable, nothing out of the norm for Merced. I opened the window to get some air and breathe.

"You think it was those two weasels?"

"Yup. I do think that. This is something bigger. I gotta get a handle on it. This might mean war. I can't explain away someone breaking in at the warehouse."

A lump formed in my throat. "I pray it's not that."

As I turned into the warehouse driveway, I saw a fire extinguisher being used and one of the security team from the alarm company on deck. Nobody else.

I scanned the street as we parked and walked swiftly toward the two men.

"Hey, Mr. Christopher is that right?" A beefy security dude with a flashlight shone it at his shoes. In his hand he was holding a bag.

"Yes. That's right. How you doin', man? What happened here?" Diego asked.

"Good, good. We responded to a call for this address," he said curtly. He shone the light at me and smiled. His light was the only source. Other than that, the whole parking lot area was pitch black. The moon was hiding behind clouds, refusing to show its face. "Looks like a small spot fire was lit just outside the building. Set off the smoke alarm for the building. Nothing major. Probably some kids around the way. Sorry you had to come out for it."

I breathed a sigh of relief but at the same time wondered who did it.

"Ah, how did the fire start? You got any clues about it?" Diego asked. I paced around the side of the building to take a look.

"Molotov cocktail. That's what I've got here." He held up the bag in his hand.

"Holy shit. People are still throwing those pieces of shit?"

"Well, that's why I say it was young kids, because this is a backyard job. Still, we're going to hold on to it and investigate. We also have the security tape. Once we roll it we will get it back to you."

"Please do. I want these bastards caught. They did a shit job if they were planning to burn down the place," Diego mused.

"They did. I don't know if they were trying to do that, more like trying to be a nuisance." The security guy wrote down some notes. "So hey, we have all your details. I will be in touch with you, Mr. Christopher, once I've had a look at the tapes."

"Can I have that cocktail? I wanna take a closer look at it."

The beefy security dude hesitated for a minute. "Are you going to take this to the cops? I suggest you do. You might want to take along the tape when we release it to you as well," he said.

"I might. Depends. Thanks for coming out."

"You're welcome, Mr. Christopher. Give me a call if you think of anything else about the issue." He held out his hand for the shake. Diego shook it back.

"Will do," Diego said grimly.

Diego curled me into him and kissed my head. We watched the security walk away. I looked down at the ground where the cocktail had been. The bottom half of the door was singed and some of the paint peeled off.

"Wow. Motherfuckers." We looked at one another.

"They didn't mean for it to go anywhere. They wanted to send a message. We are in a battle or the beginnings of it and don't even know it," Diego sighed, running a hand through his sexy bedroom hair as the furrow deepened.

"I feel like this is all my fault in a way," I sighed, looking around the building.

"How do you figure that?"

"I mean, I don't know us being together has started this."

"Honey, this started because of two dicks in a bar who are starting a prostitution ring in a gang and you refused. I'm not letting you do that." Diego grabbed my hand as we looked around inside the warehouse. Everything looked to be in order, nothing that my naked eye could pick up. "Sons of bitches. Anyway, let's get out of here. I'll be back in the morning. I'm getting Rick to have his boys stand guard here."

I shook my head and walked hand in hand with Diego to the car. All of our secret night escapade plans had been ruined. I had a sinking feeling of desperation hit in the pit of my stomach. I wanted to go back home, to see if my brother was there. If he knew anything about this shit at all. This situation triggered memories of the lifestyle I'd shared with Carlos all over again...

We reached the car in silence and Diego gave me a funny look as I got in the driver's side.

"What's wrong? You're so quiet," he said.

"I don't know, it's just a lot. I gotta get home and see what Palo knows about these guys. He has to know something," I said desperately.

"Damn right he knows something," Diego mumbled. I said nothing, which probably made the situation worse. I didn't know what to say, to be honest. We drove back in relative silence as I thought about the situation. I stopped the car in his driveway and maneuvered to look at him in the moonlight. His demeanor made him look like a dark character out of Batman.

"Look, I gotta go home now. I know you think my brother did this but he wouldn't be a part of this. I'm telling you. The quicker I can talk to him, the quicker I can get back to you."

"Misty, I don't know what to think right now. But if you're lying to me, there's going to be a different story going down. Find out. But you better do it now. Once Ryder finds out... oooweee, all hell is gonna break loose. Trust me."

DIEGO

I lay awake in my bed, listening to the sounds of the crickets outside my window. This moment felt a lot like La Playa – the old days. Worry about Misty crept into my mind. Her future and about her wanting to be a doctor. Whether I was being selfish pulling her into this lifestyle once again.

All I knew was that my body and soul ached to be with her. That was how I knew I loved her. I didn't feel like this in my marriage, and I sure as hell didn't feel like this with Crystal. I waited for her text message to come through. Twenty-five minutes later.

"I'm home safe Papi. Palo is here in the house. See I told you!"
"I'm glad you're safe. xxxooo"

For all my tough-guy bravado I still didn't have the kahunas to tell her I loved her. I looked out my window, searching for anything in the parking lot. I had no clue if they knew where I lived. This was getting beyond me now and I would need to call in the big dogs. I had no choice. There was no other way. I made up my mind and tried to go to sleep. I tossed and turned in a fitful state. I woke up in a cold sweat as I thought of the guys in my kitchen in La Playa. I wiped my brow and got up to go to the bathroom. I padded softly to the kitchen and grabbed a beer to calm the pulsating beat in my chest. I let it run down my throat as I ruminated over a game plan. Nothing came to mind quickly. I looked at the clock on the wall. Two-forty a.m.

I managed to lay my head down on my pillow and get a little rest. I woke up discombobulated. I tried to moisten my lips. My tongue was mighty dry. I turned over slowly and hung my feet over the bed to get my bearings.

I looked over at the clock. It said seven-thirty a.m, so I'd managed to get a little sleep. I took the rubber band from around my wrist and tied my shoulder-length hair back. I walked gingerly to the kitchen and poured myself a glass of water. I stood over the sink and assessed how I'd begun shoveling the dirt in my own grave. I showered and got ready fast. My instincts told me to get to the warehouse as quickly as possible for some reason. I mounted my bike and let the cool fresh morning air wake me up as I rode over. I stopped off at one of my favorite cafés and picked up a breakfast sandwich. The smell of the bacon and egg hit my nostrils, making me salivate. I bit into it, ripping it to shreds before I got back on the bike. I dropped the wrapper in the trash and kept moving. As soon as I got into the parking lot, I felt something strange. Like the day was about to be different. The front of the warehouse was a reminder of the Molotov cocktail. I planned to wipe down the soot from the door a little later. I would wait for the tape to come through from the security company to see.

I went straight to the radio to turn it on and walked around the whole building on edge. This was the second time I'd packed my Smith and Wesson. I didn't want to have to do that. But given the situation, I had no choice. I felt around my back to check it was still there and ran my hands over the smooth handle of the gun one more time. My palms were a little sweatier than I would have liked.

I couldn't shake this eerie feeling I had. I walked to the office to turn the computer on. Nothing new but a message from Ryder with a receipt for the parts I'd ordered through the clubhouse. I moved some shit around the desk in restlessness. I was like a heavyweight boxer waiting in the ring. I had the other Honda to work on, but I just looked at it. I walked to the front of the warehouse again and took a rag to wipe down the walls.

That was when I saw it. The envelope tucked right under the front door. I picked it up, slid my hand over it and flipped it over in my hand. I opened the seal and inside was a note.

Did you enjoy that little fire we sent your way?

There's more than that little spark to come if you don't pay up in the next 48 hours.

This is a message from the Las Balas crew. We need $100,000 in cash delivered in the next 48 hours. We will be calling in to check on your progress. We hope you have life insurance.

Expect a phone call from a private number. If you don't answer your warehouse will be burned down. Oh and if you don't pay we will kill you.

Yours truly Las Balas crew.

My face turned into a ball of fire as the ink jumped off the page at me. These fuckers were really trying my patience. I crouched down to stop my head from spinning. I just wanted the warehouse to stop spinning. I read over the note again. Now I had to call Ryder and the boys. This was it. I had to build the chapter quickly. I would need all hands on deck. I placed my splayed fingers on the ground and steadied myself. I let the anger wash over me. Once I gathered myself, I rose to my feet.

"Rick, hey, it's Diego. How you doing?"

"Good, buddy, what's up? I'm coming your way today. I was going to see if you wanted to catch up for a beer."

I coughed. "How 'bout you bring the beers here. I need your hands on deck. The chapter hasn't even officially opened but we got a situation."

"Uh-huh. Those dudes, right?"

"Yeah, how'd you know?"

"I been in security for a long time, I thought they might have been casing the joint. What's the verdict?"

"You're more than right. They got a ransom on my head."

"Holy fucking shit! Do you know why?"

"Las Balas crew. I have a fair idea. Get here when you can. I could use a helping hand on the ground."

"I got you, and I got a group of guys that can help us out," Rick said. "Let me get off the phone so I can round them up. We can case the perimeter on guard until we catch these suckers. Give me twenty. I would start setting up barricades if I were you. Put blocks over the window so they can't see in. Is the property insured?"

"Property's insured and that's a good start with the barricades. See you when you get here."

I set to work with the spare MDF panels at the back of the warehouse. I carried them out from the back storeroom and to the first of the back windows to check the sizing match. Actually perfect. It was as if they were made to be boarded up anyway.

I grabbed the nailgun from my toolbox and set to work on each window. I kept my ears tuned for cars on the street, leaving one of the windows clear while I was inside so I could see out. I felt around for my gun and took it out of the holster and set it down on the table in front of me. The deafening roar of my heartbeat in my throat made it hard to breathe. The problem was I had no idea when the strike would happen. I had just about finished setting the boards when I heard the low hum of a car engine. I snatched my gun off the table and pinned myself along the side of the wall of the warehouse. I kept my voice still and my breath steady. I waited for the person to answer.

"Diego," they called out, banging on the front door. "Diego, it's me, Rick." Beads of sweat had formed on my forehead. I jogged to the front door, gun in hand, and slid the door back.

Rick took one look at my face and the gun and said, "Holy shit."

"Yeah, pretty much. I'm sweating bullets here."

Rick beckoned to me and he had a four-pack of beer. "Let's sit, form a game plan to win this."

"Okay." I pushed the loose strands back from my face as I sat across from him. He had a stern demeanor and was wearing all black.

"Okay. So what I didn't explain to you is that I own a security company – it's small. I do the weekend stuff for extra cash. If you want to hire me to run security I can and quit that. I spoke to Ryder and I'm going to come in and train the enforcers with a new bag of tricks."

I gave him a handshake. "Sounds good."

"Got the letter? Can we get this to the cops?"

"No. Cops are on payroll and pick sides. Plus, they would much rather we kill one another."

Rick grimaced and twisted the top of a beer and handed it to me. "Here, drink up. Tell me more about the ransom and more importantly, does the club have the capital?"

I winced. "Yeah, we got it, they know that."

"Okay, so what game are they running?"

"Two of the Las Balas crew are running a pro' ring and they want to fund the operation. Apparently, these two are working alone. They were apparently kicked out of Las Balas. I'm not convinced."

Rick looked confused. "Wait a minute. They are blackmailing you under the guise of Las Balas but they're not part of the chapter?"

I sucked down part of the beer and stared at Rick. "Yep. That's what I'm saying. The problem is, I don't know whether to believe that or not. The source I'm not sure is credible yet. I have definite intel that the Las Balas boys like their pro's so they're seeking to profit off them."

"Ahhhh. Okay, big business with brothels, maybe that's what they're trying to set up. There's a few underground ones. Where the red lights are on, you know what I mean?"

"Yeah, I do." The edge was off now that Rick was in the picture.

"Okay. I will call in my guys to case the perimeter. They got semi-automatics. I have some camera gear as well, right in my car. Will take me a couple of hours to test and set up."

"We already have a camera."

Rick pointed to the inside. "You need a camera for the inside panel so you can see out the front who is coming in. I can set it up on the computer and wire it. You also need a camera around the back. All sides."

"Okay. I gotta call Ryder too. I need him to check negotiations between Palo and us. He needs to know now." I let the last of the beer slide down. I kept repeating myself about Ryder. But first I wanted to tell Misty...

"Looks like things are getting pretty real, huh?"

"Doesn't get much realer. I didn't come here for this, but we gotta defend our territory."

Rick pointed to the banner on the side of the wall. "That's the code. I guess I'm putting it to the test now."

"You sure are. Welcome to being an Outlaw."

"Proud to be in. Let's do this."

MISTY

My hair sat on top of my head like a bird's nest and I hadn't been to class for the last two days. My nerves were shot and now my own brother was looking at me like the enemy.

"So you heading to class today?" he asked innocently as I made my morning coffee.

"I'm not feeling too good today, so I think I'm going to just stay home."

"Uh-huh. Are you coming down with something?"

"Yeah, I might be." I averted my eyes from his and moved past him with my coffee to the bedroom. I didn't have any major tests, but Shauna was texting me like crazy.

"Girl where have you been? I missed you yesterday. You good?"
"I'm fine, I'm just not feeling good."
"Really? Want me to bring you some chicken soup?"
"No I'm ok thank you see you tomorrow"
"Ok well get better xx"

The guilt ate at me a little. I knew ultimately I could talk to Shauna, but something made me pull back. I texted Diego so Palo, the sneaky bastard wouldn't hear me on the phone. I let my fingers do the typing.

"Hey are you ok. I'm worried."

"Call you later gotta handle some things."

I frowned and lay back on the bed with my hands over my chest. My heart was ka-booming out of it. My central nervous system felt like it was about to explode. I tried to get up and clean my room. I tried to sit and say a prayer to Santa Maria. It didn't work. Nothing was working. Thirty agonizing minutes passed.

"Hey, baby." A flat-sounding Diego had finally called.

"Hey, honey. I don't know why I had this bad feeling. I might be paranoid." I kept my panicked voice low.

"You're not."

"I'm not what?" I was confused.

"Paranoid. Those guys in black came back and they left a letter."

I stood up quickly "They what!" I hissed under my breath. "Hold on. I'm going outside." I snuck out of my room in the backyard.

"Yeah. I got a ransom note for a hundred thou' in forty-eight hours," he told me.

"I don't understand. Why the hell would they do that?" I threw my hand up to the sky in disbelief.

"Our guess is they are using it to start a brothel. I gotta get the boys involved now."

"Oh my God. This is bad, isn't it?" I clutched my forehead and my breath started to pick up in pace.

"I mean, yeah. The note was signed by Las Balas. So either your brother is involved or he has no idea. Which is it, Misty?"

"Diego. Palo wouldn't do this. Give me some time to get the names. I'm telling you. They are not even on the club page."

"I don't exactly know that. All I know is we got serious beef and I'm putting security in place. May not be a good idea to see one another until this blows over. I gotta deal with this."

My stomach somersaulted as I thought about my involvement.

"I swear to you, baby. Palo is a good guy."

I nearly jumped right out of my skin. Palo was behind me and had snuck up without me knowing.

"I fucking take it back. You sneaking up on me, now estúpido!" I pushed him in the chest to his surprise. He caught my hand and turned my wrist a little. "Palo, let go!" I hung up the phone quickly.

"Why are you so jumpy lately? What aren't you telling me, Misty?" Palo's eyes burned straight through me and we were inches from one another. I wondered if he could smell the fear in me. I stepped aside from him and he dropped my arm.

"Move, Palo! Don't eavesdrop on my conversations!"

He watched me storm past him and back into the house.

"It's my house. I will do whatever I want," he yelled as I slammed the door. I waited for him to follow me, but I didn't hear his footsteps.

I went into my room and put on my sneakers. I wanted to ride out so I could clear my head and see how to clear my knucklehead brother's name. I came out of the room steaming with anger, but I had forgotten my car keys, so I swung around and went back into my room.

"What the hell is going on with you, Misty?" He stepped in front of me on the way out.

"You are overbearing, that's what's wrong. I need some air and it's time for me to get out."

"I know you're still seeing him. My sources saw you," Palo said in an eerily calm voice. I stopped. My hair had flown all around my face. *Does he know about the ransom note? Could my brother have done it?*

"Okay. Let me call your bluff, big brother. Who told you? How do you know?"

"I have eyes and ears all over Merced. We are Las Balas. I make it my business to know." He gave me a sinister smile as his eyes hooded over.

"Palo, tell me you're not involved in any criminal activity with Las Balas," I said with a deathly tone.

"What? We got rid of all the criminals. I told you I'm cleaning up the chapter." He looked at me weirdly.

"Tell me who they were, Palo. Those two guys. I wanna know their names. Tell me! I demand that you tell me now!" I slammed my flat palm on the kitchen bench. Palo looked me over without blinking.

"I ran them out of town, therefore you don't need to know. Besides, what the fuck are you gonna do?" he threatened, his eyes full of misplaced anger.

"Yes, I do need to know and a lot can be done." I pinched my fingers together in front of his face.

"Why? I told you I handled it and what – you don't believe me?" he spat out, his eyes glowing with rage.

I twisted up my lips and pierced him with my eyes. "Yep, just like you believe me about Diego, right?"

Palo's face went beet red. "That's not the same. The guy's a safety risk and it's not a good idea."

"Why isn't it? Why do gangs have to be rivals? Why is it they can't just be connected? Since you're so community-minded and all…" I jutted out my chin at him and stood sideways. I had silenced my brother. At least for the minute, anyway.

"Look, I'm going to get to the bottom of it. Let me handle things, it's definitely too dangerous for you to be involved. Don't even think about doing a goddamn thing." Palo's stern voice meant business as he pointed his finger at me. I watched as his small compact body stormed away and walked inside. I followed closely behind him. He grabbed his jacket from the couch out front without turning around. He lifted two fingers as a departing salute.

"I'll be back later. I gotta take care of a few things."

"I bet," I punched out as he closed the front door.

I licked my lips and put two hands to my temples, breathing out an anxious breath. I looked around aimlessly for a minute as I worked out what to do next. Instinctively, I moved to the study where Palo worked from home sometimes. He had computer drives and IT discs and hardware stacked everywhere. I went into the office and shuffled the loose papers on the desk around, looking for clues. Anything that might be a lead to the names of two deathlords. Too many pieces of paper. Palo was a messy dude. I stepped back and looked at the desk. Where would I hide the details of two former chapter members? I pulled the two drawers open on the left. My heart pounded in my chest. If Palo walked back in the door, I would be dead meat. Top drawer, I stared at paper clips, a box of matches, pencils, tape and other stationery items. I pulled out the second drawer. A small notepad with two names on it. I held it in my hands and stared until the names forged in ink blurred from my gaze.

Jimmy Santos and Blaze Hernandez. Shakily I removed the notepad and took it with me to my room. I closed the door and switched on my laptop. Felt like a million years before my laptop loaded up.

"Come on," I muttered to myself. I typed in both names. The shock of what I found made me want to vomit. The fat guy I saw at the club that approached me was part of an article. Jimmy Santos from Merced sentenced to two years' jail for the sexual assault of an underaged minor. I clicked on images and yep, that was him. I clutched my stomach and forced myself not to hurl.

I clicked out and made myself keep looking on the internet. I typed Blaze Hernandez's name in the search bar. No criminal records or charges that came up but images came up with none other than El Diablo. The depth of darkness in their eyes was hard to describe, but it permeated both their faces. The image came from Facebook. I clicked on it and it led to Blaze's Facebook page. Tempted, I hovered the mouse over his name but didn't click. I was in half a mind to bait the guy and create a fake page to corner him. I closed my eyes as my legs shook under the table. *That might be the only way to draw them out and distract them from coming after Diego.* I decided to call him. I peeked out my door again to check Palo wasn't there. Only the whirring of the fan he left on in the front room. I walked down the hallway and turned it off.

I walked back to my room with my legs wobbly. I picked up my phone and dialed Diego.

He answered on the fifth ring. "Hullo?"

"Hey, baby. I have some news." My mouth was dry like cotton.

"What news do you have?" His voice sounded tired and suspicious.

"I got the names of the two guys. Hopefully your crew knows them. But I have a solution if you let me get involved."

Diego huffed on the other end of the line. "Mamacita! I told you no. Give me the names and we'll take it from here. I gotta get in touch with Ryder, it's gone too far anyway."

"The names are Jimmy Santos and Blaze Hernandez."

Diego fell silent for a moment. "Jimmy Santos, Jimmy Santos... Why does that name sound familiar? I know that name..."

"He was brought up and convicted of sexual assault charges when he was younger. Served time in juvie from what I read."

"Fuck! I should have known. That was the thirteen-year-old girl. Yoda told me about that a while back when we were at war with Las Balas. Shit's making sense now. I gotta get rid of these fuckers. Get 'em off the motherfucking streets. I don't want you near this. You hear me?"

"I know. Same thing my brother said." I sighed helplessly.

"What? What is your brother doing?"

"Well, he said he took care of it. Obviously he didn't. I was thinking I could set up a fake profile picture or something and catfish one of them. Should be easy enough and lure them into the open. You can handle it from there. That's what I was going to suggest. You don't have much time to waste, papi." I realized I was biting my nails, so I dropped my hand from my mouth.

"I don't even want to tell you it's not like I haven't been through this before because I have. We got it covered. But that's not a bad idea. I spoke to the pro' who knows who was setting it up and they were hanging around The Partition. Just might work. I want you to stay out of it. Thanks for the names. Let me work on it."

"Okay. Please be careful. I feel- I feel like this is my fault." I felt the tears welling up in my eyes.

"Baby, like I said, it's not your fault. Are you kidding me? I'm not going to let anything happen to you," he said fiercely. "Besides, I love you. It's too late now."

"You love me?" I let the words sink in. "I love you too, Diego. Please be safe."

"I will. I promise."

DIEGO

I shook out my shoulders, the knots forming in quick succession once I got off the call with Misty. I shook out my hands and opened my fridge as normal. I looked at the beers, closed it shut and re-opened it again, pulling one out. The whooshing sound let off as I popped the beer open.

I sucked it down until one-third of it was gone. Didn't ease the nerves. I peeked through my Venetian blinds to see if anyone was in the parking lot. Not a single person in sight. Only the sound of an owl hooting in the background. I closed the door. I had my laptop in my bedroom. I went in there and scrounged around for it. I rarely looked at it unless I needed to. I bent down under my bed and slid it out. I remembered I left it there in a laptop bag. I fired it up while I sat on the bed. Time to research. I wanted to soak up as much information about these clowns as I could. I needed to find someone in the know to lure them out. Misty's plan wasn't half bad.

Jimmy Santos. I clicked on the article from the local Merced News.

A local teenager has been charged with the sexual assault of a *minor whose name will remain undisclosed. Bail is set at $15,000.* A corresponding picture with the fat fucker sat at the top of the article. He was fat as a teenager too. From the moment I saw him in my parking lot of the warehouse, I knew he was trouble. His side profile in the mugshot screamed of a deviant. I switched out and looked up Blaze Hernandez. There were plenty of photos of him floating across the net. One with his arm around fellow weasel El Diablo. I should have known. Both of them were wearing their chapter patches on their leather jackets. I now understood that it was out of my hands. It was time to call in the Outlaws. To be, well, Outlaws.

I walked with my bare feet out to the kitchen like I always did. I picked up my cell phone as I jumped off the seesaw of indecision.

"Hey, Diego. Midnight caller, huh? This has gotta be good, right?" Ryder's answered.

"Yeah, it is. You're gonna love it," I replied sarcastically.

"Okay, hit me with it," Ryder said as I heard him moving around the background.

"Las Balas left me a nice little note. I got a ransom on my head for a hundred thousand."

"Those muthafuckin' bastards." The anger in Ryder's voice was evident. I checked out as I sipped my beer. Misty flashed through my mind. There was no way she could be in on this. The way she fed the information to me on the phone. The panic and the careful nature of her tone. What a way to declare our love for one another.

"So what's the plan? There's no way we're paying the bastards. We have to outsmart them," I probed Ryder.

"Easy. We're going to war. I have to set the example now I'm president. Did they see reason? No. So then we ain't backing down either." Ryder's sleepy voice sprang to life.

I looked out my window from the kitchen. Merced, outside of the city limits, reminded me of the desert a little and our sojourn down to Tijuana. Wrong time to be thinking about that, but I needed a happy memory. I switched back to the conversation.

"I found both their profiles online. Jimmy Santos and Blaze Hernandez. You know 'em?"

"Yeah, I know both those cretins. We can take 'em down easy."

"A few other things..." I cringed as I launched all that was hidden. "I'm pretty sure I got a visit from them earlier in the week, with a small fire at the warehouse. They were harassing Misty too."

"Misty? What the fuck has she got to do with this? I thought I told you the girl was bad news and to stay the hell away from her?" Ryder sounded like an angry father chastising his kid.

I drained the last of my beer and sighed. "Ryder, they harassed her, she ain't got nothing to do with these two. Keep her out of it. Both of these guys are trying to start a pro' ring. I met a pro' who told me they tried to pimp her."

"You were holding all this?" Ryder's voice was in full command now. He meant business.

"I did, but I thought I could handle it and it wasn't going anywhere."

"Diego, this is what the chapter is for. To lean on. I'm gathering the boys and we are riding in tomorrow morning. What's the next instruction for the ransom?"

"I mean, I don't even know if it's legitimate, first off."

"Oh, it's legitimate. Las Balas don't declare anything unless it is. They wouldn't have sent that to you if it wasn't."

"There's a divide in the chapter though, Ryder. I don't know that all of Las Balas is in on this." As the words flew out of my mouth I wondered how it came to be that I was advocating for Las Balas.

"You chickenshit. You're bigging them up now? Diego,

that girl has got you twisted. She's probably a mole sent to infiltrate the chapter set-up."

I felt the anger flowing through me the more Ryder brought Misty up. I would stand for her no matter what, I realized. I would have to trust her in this situation. "Leave her out of it, Ryder."

"We don't have long to set this up. If I need to set the wheels in motion, I'm going to let them know we're coming for 'em."

"No surprise tactics?"

"We could rush the chapter, yeah, but I gotta see how we're going to work this. Be ready. I'm calling the boys now. We'll be near your place at sunrise or thereabouts. I need maps if you have them. I need a location for the pro' you met too. I need to see if we can get in touch with what they're doing. We are coming in strapped. Be ready, Diego."

"Okay" was all I could manage to get out before the phone clicked dead. My stomach dropped. I didn't want a chapter war. I came to Merced to get away from that shit. I couldn't go back to sleep. My mind was racing and I was too wired.

Las Balas headquarters were situated at the back of Merced toward the airport. From what I heard, the clubhouse was relatively small. I pulled out one of the Merced maps from my kitchen drawer that I picked up at the Information Center in town. I thought back to last time Outlaw Souls raided a chapter. It was a long time ago and I hadn't been part of it.

"Moves had to put a stop to a few things. Las Balas was trying to steal from us. He put a few clips in their crew." Yoda had relayed the tale over a few drinks at Blue Dog Saloon.

"What happened to Moves? I never talked to him about it."

"He got hit. A few of the other guys had to back him up. We lost two in the fight, but at least Las Balas knew we were a force. That they couldn't fuck with us. Ryder was there too."

"Man, that's crazy," I mumbled.

"Sure was a crazy time, but Padre set it straight and it came to a mutual truce between us as gangs. But we've always had a little beef with them. We've always been ready to strike if necessary. I wouldn't trust Las Balas as far I could throw them," Yoda lamented.

That was then and this was now. Ready to go to war again. I wanted Misty to be safe. My body and mind were torn. I wanted her with me so I could protect her if what she said was true. On the other hand, I wanted her away from me so she wouldn't be a part of what was going on.

Hours passed as I ran the checklist of possibilities through my mind. None of them included giving these suckers the money. Looking at them online, I would take my chances that both of them would fold under pressure. To me they were amateurs.

The promise of daylight broke through around five a.m. The navy-blue sky lifted to slate-gray as I poured a cup of coffee and waited for Ryder to arrive. The almighty purr of the motorcycle engines came through, lifting me from my erratic thoughts. Three loud thumps sounded off at the door. Grim-faced, I rose from the kitchen table and opened the door. Ryder with his wiry build and mangy beard was equally grim-faced.

"Hey, wassup, man." Ryder dapped me with a tap on the back. Yoda, Trainer, Moves and Vlad walked in. If Vlad and Moves were here, then I knew it was serious business.

Vlad stood an imposing figure at six-feet-five, tattoo sleeves running the length of both of his arms, stopping at the wrists. He was heavily muscled from top to bottom, taking up most of the door frame when he entered. He dapped me after Ryder and entered my house, making it look small. Even his face was muscled and his eyes held the energy of a killer.

"Vlad. How you doin', man?"

"Good, good." A man of few words, he looked around my place and peeked his head around the corners. "Nice place, man. Good for you, you come here. We got some business to take care of, huh?" Vlad gestured in his disjointed Russian accent.

I kneaded the muscles at the back of my neck. "Looks like it. A ransom is on my head."

Vlad nodded and looked to Ryder. "Can we pay?" Obviously Vlad hadn't been briefed on the non-payment arrangement.

Ryder shook his legs out from the ride. "No. We ain't paying shit, Vlad." The defiance in his booming voice made it ultra-clear. Vlad nodded in respect at the answer.

"Where can we get breakfast around here? Let's talk." Ryder switched the subject swiftly.

"Up a little further they got breakfast spots, or close to the warehouse. If we head there, we can keep an eye on things better."

"You're right," Yoda said. He was already at the door, ready to go.

I grabbed my jacket from the couch and led the guys back out the door.

Ryder pulled a cigarette from his pocket and put it in his mouth, cupping his hands around it as he used his lighter to spark up. He took a puff and the smoke released from his nostrils like a dragon.

Vlad put his fists together. "I got a nice knuckle sandwich for these fucks if they try it."

Moves chuckled as he headed over to his black, sleek Harley. His motorbike was custom-fit just for him. His bike was laced with shiny black chrome with a Jaguar spray-painted on the side.

Ryder slid his helmet on and looked at me. "Lead the way, brother."

I signaled and all engines purred at once as we headed to my favorite breakfast spot. We hit the road and pulled up in the gravel parking lot. A few people came out of the diner and stared at us heavy. We all ignored them. I swung in the door first and headed to the counter.

"Hey, Marcelle, how you doin' this morning?"

"We good. How are you, Diego? I see you brought your crew with you. Big boys. Time to eat, I see." Marcelle was an older Spanish lady who cooked a mean bacon and egg sandwich. Not too bad with the pancakes as well. I turned sideways and all the boys were looking at the menu up above.

"Yes, time to eat," I replied simply.

We pulled up at the biggest booth and started talking strategy.

I spoke first. "Look, this might not be Las Balas. There's a possibility these two are operating by themselves on the fly. They're just using the Las Balas name."

Ryder replied gruffly, "How do you know that?" Marcelle came out with two jugs of juice and put them in the middle of the table.

"Sources. These guys apparently got kicked out of Las Balas. So you don't want to start a war for no reason."

Yoda made a strange face at me. "Well, no, we don't want to start a war. But you got a ransom on your head so we can't just sit here and let that happen."

Moves coughed and stepped in. "We can case the joint and leave a warning to see how they respond. If we're going to do that, we gotta do it today. You got until tomorrow, right?"

Ryder tapped Moves. "Let's get to the warehouse. You haven't even heard from these guys, right? I mean, they haven't even given you the next steps for instruction. They don't sound organized. If they were with Las Balas, this would be coming a different way. It's not like them. I mean, we didn't exactly sit down and have cups of tea last time but they sure as hell ran it a lot smoother."

Marcelle dropped a plate with egg and bacon sandwiches for everyone at the table. All of them were wrapped in brown lunch paper covering. I unraveled mine and sank my teeth in. The runny egg yolk ran out onto the table. I cleared it up with a napkin.

"We can send a warning shot. That's what we need to do," Vlad said. "That way we know if those punk-ass bitches are operating separately." He devoured his egg and bacon sandwich in about two bites. He flagged Marcelle from afar and pointed to his sandwich.

"You want another one?" she called from the front counter.

"Yes, ma'am, these are delicious." Vlad had a big grin on his face. He was a big softie unless he was hunting you down.

"Vlad, let's get it to go. We got work to do," Ryder said before turning back to me. "Do they have your number? Have these clowns attempted to call you?"

"No, no phone contact, they just dropped off the letter and said to wait for the next contact." Ryder turned over his fingers on his hand and looked at them. He wore a jade ring. Never saw him once without it. Must have meant something to him.

"Huh. So if I'm right and they came twice to the warehouse, then they will have a present there when we arrive. You said they tried to scare you with the fire situation. So let's be prepared when we ride in."

Every one of the boys looked to Ryder and nodded in

agreement. The war was starting and I was powerless to stop it.

Marcelle came to the table and pushed the egg and bacon sandwich into Vlad's large hands.

"Thank you. How much?"

"Nothing for you. On the house." She winked at him and nodded her head out the window. "Come back more often, you're good for business, fellas." A crowd of people had stopped outside, taking a look at the pimped-out bikes in the parking lot and whispering.

We all laughed.

"Will do." Vlad's eyes opened and he high-fived Marcelle. She laughed and wiped her hands on her apron.

"Guys, let's head to the warehouse." I summoned the crew to get a move on. My head was telling me that news was at the other end. We looked like a football team putting on our helmets. Cars beeped as they went past. I led the charge out to the warehouse. I idled as we reached the edge of the parking lot. From a distance, everything looked to be in order. I let Moves and Vlad in front. They crept in and parked right out front of the warehouse. Both of them dismounted off their bikes and pulled their pieces from under their waistbands. Two imposing hulks casing the warehouse. We waited at the entrance. Minutes later, both of them beckoned, letting Yoda, Ryder and me know the coast was clear for us to come forward. I dismounted.

Vlad with his tight jaw said, "Lead the way." I nodded and pressed the alarm code on the wall and unlocked the front door. I flicked on all the lights. Vlad and Moves stepped past me and slid along the perimeter on each side with their guns raised. The air held tension. Something made me look down. Another letter. *These guys like to use their pens. I'm surprised they're smart enough to be able to write.*

I picked it up. Ryder and Yoda watched in anticipation.

The envelope had some weight to it. I opened it up. Inside was a cheap prepaid phone and a note.

Use this phone. We will contact you on it. You now have 24 hours to get our money. We assume you have it by now. We want you to pack a garbage bag with the full funds in $100,000 bundles at Fahrens Park entrance. On the way in is a garbage can. Drop the money in there at 23 hundred hours. Come alone. If you don't we'll kill you and execute phase two of our plan. You've been warned.

Ryder waited patiently until I finished the letter. I handed it to him. His eyes scanned through at a quick speed. I watched as he passed it to Yoda.

Vlad and Moves anticipated the next set of instructions.

"So it looks like these guys think they are some kind of mafia dudes. We ain't gonna play around with them. I say we bum-rush their chapter beforehand. If we give them this ransom, then they will keep extorting us. This can't be Las Balas, they play the game better than this. I think you might be right, Diego. These clowns are solo. If they are, we are in luck and will squash both of them like the disgusting rodents they are." One side of Ryder's face curled up in a snarl so nasty it even made me step back a little. I breathed out. *Might be one small step.*

"We will back you up when you go out, Diego. You're not going out there alone. We can drop a bag of fake money in there. These guys are full of shit."

I stood there, thinking about it. The whole thing didn't make sense. "It's like they want us to start a war with Las Balas." I rifled my hands through the tangles in my hair. "I say we call their bluff and I go out and dump the bag like Vlad said." I stared at Ryder, waiting for a response. "What would be even better is if we can get a source to help us locate these punks." I tapped Ryder as he paced the warehouse. "We got the new sign-up as well and he has a security crew. Maybe swear him in as the Merced Enforcer. We can get them to set some traps up at Fahren."

Ryder stroked his beard. "That's a plan I like. Get them on the phone, set it up." His eyes glistened as his mouth moved to a smile. "Time to get down and dirty in Merced."

MISTY

The dark of my room made me feel suffocated so I got up and snuck into the kitchen and turned the light on. The ticking of the clock sounded like death's doorknock to me. By now, Diego had just over twenty-four hours left to go before he had to deliver the ransom. Jimmy and Blaze, what a combination. I hadn't heard from Diego in a day, and the worry was gnawing away at me, slowly but surely. I had school tomorrow, but it didn't matter. The last few days had been a blurry mess of lectures and staring off into space.

I wondered if a calming cup of tea might settle my nerves. I boiled some water on the stove and waited for it to whistle. No sound came from the other end of the house, but I knew Palo was here. I peeped out and down the hallway. The light was on in the office. The pot whistled and I threw a tea bag in and let the water trickle into the cup. I heard my phone beep and my stomach jumped a little. I quickly poured and went back to my room. I looked at the blue screen.

"Give your brother the heads-up. The chapter might get raided. I'm trying to redirect. Call you later k."

I nearly dropped my cup. Some of the water splashed on

my hand as I read the message again. *Shit.* I had to come up with something quick.

"*K. Can you talk?*"

"*Yeah I got a few.*"

I rang his phone and sucked in a deep breath.

"Hey, papi."

"Hey, mama. How you holding up?"

"I'm not. I'm worried sick."

"I know. Listen, I'm trying my best. I don't think they will. I know those dweebs are trying to start the war and get the money."

"They are. If I can get my bro' to concentrate on finding them. I will. I have a plan."

"Babe," he pleaded.

"No, wait. Hear me out. I'm going to tell Palo they're following me. That way he can work on finding them. I can find out where they live. I can let you know," I begged Diego.

"Hmm. Might work, is he there?"

"Yep. He's in the office. I'm going to talk to him. I'll text you."

"Baby, be careful. I don't want this backfiring."

"If Outlaw Souls start a war...what's going to happen between us? We have to stop it!" I cried. "We'll never make it." Short breaths made it hard for me to get my words out.

"That's my girl. Okay. Make it work. I'll do what I can on my end. Keep me posted."

"Diego. Please stay safe. I love you."

"I love you too, lil' mama." The phone clicked off and I walked out to see Palo. As I approached the door, I heard him talking on the phone.

"The warehouse is at the back of Merced? Okay. That's it. Time for a visit from Las Balas. Nobody messes with my sister." I coughed loudly so he could hear me and watched him nearly fly out of his chair. The seat moved under him and he had to place his two hands on the table to regain stability. I just looked at his bald head. "How much did you hear?"

"All of it. I need to talk to you about something."

He pointed to the spare chair in the office. "Have a seat."

"I know who the two guys are."

Palo's two hands were in the shape of a triangle as he pressed his fingertips together. His brow was furrowed into a V shape, looking at me. "No shit."

I rolled my eyes at him. "I mean Jimmy and Blaze, right? They aren't gone. You didn't do your job. They're still following me." I cringed slightly as I watched my brother's face. It was so hard to lie to him. I wondered if I should have just told him the truth. Too late now, I was already trapped in the lie.

"What the fuck! How? What did they say?" He sprayed spit towards me and it landed on my leg. I wiped it off quickly.

I licked my lips and said to him, "They threatened to follow me to campus. I looked them up. Why didn't you tell me Jimmy Santos had a record for sexual assault? Now he's after me?" I pointed to myself.

My brother looked down at his hands in guilt. "I didn't think you needed to know that."

"How the fuck didn't you think I needed to know? Where are they staying? Who did you get to run them out of town?" I pressed him.

"Aww, shit. I got our Enforcer to talk to them. Rodriguez."

"Talk?" I pressed my finger into the table and widened my eyes. "Talk? That's all you did?"

"Yeah, I know. I know. I should have been tougher. I didn't want any more bloodshed."

"So now they're still here and you're willing to let something happen to me? All because you didn't settle the score with these guys. Both of them are straight-up, low-level criminals," I spat at him. I was laying it on thick but I didn't care. I needed the point to get across.

He paused and read the distress on my face. He put his hands up in defense. "All right. You think Rodriguez might be in on it?"

"I don't fucking know, but I do know they have a black pick-up truck and I'm pretty sure they've been tailing me. That teardrop fatty had was a gang symbol. Maybe he got that in jail or something. Where did they used to live?"

"Back behind the airport, close by the chapter. Bear Creek Road or something like that. Doubt if they'll stay there now."

I slapped my brother on the leg. "You're shit! You're trying to rebuild a crime, sex-ridden motorcycle gang and make it fucking wholesome! That shit ain't for you! You're not built for it! You needed to handle this shit firsthand. Make them pay. Rodriguez punked you. He did nothing. Now, these guys are making a mockery of the chapter," I fired back and I knew my face was red. I let him have it. I watched as his face grew redder and redder, because all that I said was true. He hadn't followed the protocol.

"Shut up! I need to think. Get out of here. I need to get Rodriguez on the phone." His smoldering anger was evident, but he couldn't dispute what I said.

"You better." I folded my arms over my chest while I waited for him to make the call.

"Get out. I need some privacy." He waved me off.

I rose up from my seat. "I'll be in my room. Let me know what you're going to do," I said. Not one mention of Diego. *Good*. He was more focused on protecting me. *Okay, so they were last seen near the chapter grounds*. It was a long shot, but maybe it would help Diego.

I texted him with quick fingers as I closed my bedroom door behind me.

"Off your case for now. Bear Creek Road for Jimmy and Blaze."
Ten seconds later...
"Thanks baby."
"Are your crew staying with you?"
"No. Close by. Hotel. Why?"
"Just wanted to know. Bye."
"Ok. Call you in the morning. Dream of me."
"I will. Look forward to being in your bed soon."

What had I become? A gang member's girlfriend? Again? I sat at my study table and looked at my anatomy books. I was crisscrossed between two worlds. My heart was beating out of my chest. His biker friends were at a hotel. I wanted to go to him. I had to see him. I wanted to taste his lips. I knew it was crazy dangerous. My brain wouldn't let me think too hard. I scooted back from my chair and pulled out my night bag. I packed a few clothes in it recklessly.

I slipped out to the bathroom and grabbed my toothbrush. I washed my face and looked long and hard in the mirror. I had to fight for my man. I heard Palo yelling from the other room.

"Rodriguez! I told you to fucking handle it! I don't want smut on our name. We're not doing this anymore. My family is in danger. Fix it! Tail them and get them the fuck outta here! Especially Jimmy! That fucker is on his last year of parole. If he gets busted for a minor traffic infraction he goes back to jail. Do it and do it now!"

I held my hand to my chest. I ran out of the bathroom and back to my room. Palo would be coming down here. As soon as he left I was going to Diego. Come hell or high water.

"Misty!" Palo called out.

I stepped out of my bedroom door. I shouted back. "What you got, Palo?"

"It's done. Rodriguez is going there now. He knows now. I promise you it's done. No more bullshit."

"It better be."

Palo cracked his knuckles and rubbed his head. "'Kay. I'm going to bed. Don't disturb me. I've had enough for one day."

I sighed and scooted back to the room. My brother wasn't a killer. He didn't have it in him. He was a great hustler, businessman and possessed the gift of the gab. That was why he was club president. No other reason. He didn't have a killer instinct. I had more of it than him. I put my hair up in a tight bun and hiked my night bag over my shoulder. I knew he would hear the car leaving. But the thing was, Palo wasn't the boss of me. I had my own life and he couldn't stop me. I slipped out the back door and clicked it locked behind me. I jumped in the driver's seat and cranked the engine. My knees jiggled from excitement as adrenaline flushed through me. I felt like a real Puerto Rican bad bitch. I screeched out of the driveway and hit the freeway to Diego's house. I pulled up twenty minutes later. I saw him peep through his Venetian blinds. He opened the door a crack before I got there. I knocked three times as I let the cold night air run through my lungs.

"Special delivery. You like Puerto Rican food?"

"It's my favorite," a husky Argentine voice answered and he opened the door wide. Diego stood bare-chested, with hungry, hooded eyes. His shoulders looked broader, his hair hung in his eyes, and his biceps rippled. Low-slung jeans hugged his hips. The V of his abdominal muscles was prominent. He reeled me in with both hands and pressed me hard against the wall. The breath whooshed out of me. He ravished my mouth and I groaned into his. Our tongues chased one another as I drank him in. My hands automatically stretched around his neck. My leg raised and wrapped around him. He cupped under my buttocks and pressed his throbbing manhood into me.

"Oh, baby, what a greeting. Damn. I missed you, Misty. So

so much." A low groan rattled from his throat as he breathed life into me with his passion. No time for kissing, only time for feeling. I reached my hands down to the V line and ran my fingers there. He caught my fingers with his and unbuttoned his jeans as he breathed into the side of my neck and began to nuzzle. He drew back and looked at my face. "Let me see you." I was busy trying to catch my breath. Dazzled in a good way. My high ponytail was starting to slip. I stopped trying to hold it up and shook my hair free, letting my long hair cascade around my shoulders. "That's better," he murmured in awe. I turned on my secret weapon, my bedroom eyes. He picked me up in his thickly muscled arms and carried me to the bedroom. He didn't play around; he stepped out of his jeans and slipped my top over my head. I wriggled out of my jeans and prepared for the onslaught of sensation. Diego didn't disappoint. He curved his hands around my buttocks as I leaned into the heat. I ran the pads of my fingers in circles around his chest. He shuddered as I noticed his hair catching in line with the sliver of light through the curtain.

The room was ablaze with the flame of our heartbeats. He moved his hands up the length of my spine and rested them in the silkiness of my hair. My body was lit up from the inside through his touch. I felt the power of his engine as his arousal crushed into my leg. I slid backward on the bed and Diego followed. He unclasped my bra and began the slow, painful, ecstatic nibbling of my neck and my swollen breasts. His touch led him all the way to the garden of Eden. He slipped me out of my panties and threw them to the side. I opened myself to him, needing him to fan the flame burning in my nether regions. Our breathing matched in heaviness, the wanton desire in both of us threatening to do us in. He gave it to me. His mouth soothed the aching want as he searched through the crevices of my lips. I moaned with the longing of being away from him so long. His tongue made inroads into the electric current of my erogenous zones. His mouth clamped down into the center of me as I raised my hips in anticipation. I gasped and he grunted with satisfaction as the pulses of orgasm reigned supreme through my body. I cried out and caught a glimpse of a sensual smile curved on his lips.

He dropped out of his underwear as I enjoyed the Spanish volcano erupting between us. His manhood stood like a flagpole. I licked my lips in anticipation. He climbed on top, kneeling as if praying, his hair hanging in his eyes. Never more sexy. I admired the broadness and sheer raw power of the man in front of me. Diego tapped his hands on the top part of his chest, indicating for me to wrap my legs around him for wider entry, and I did. I watched Diego's chest rise and fall as he slid his hot cock into my core. My walls expanded to meet him. The pace was a mixture of slow grind and earthy pounding. I dug my nails into his chest as he stretched me around him further. The veins in his neck grew larger along with the hardness of his length as he pistoned in and out of me, getting closer to being extinguished by the flame of rapture.

"Yes, papi!" I cried out, clutching the stark white sheets. The low roar of a lion came from Diego's mouth as he let go and I felt the sweet slickness of my body drive him to orgasm. I wasn't far behind as the waves of heat washed over me again and again. He slowly lowered my legs and slid in the sheets beside me. He lay on his back and breathed out. I giggled and he put one hand behind his head.

"You are..." He looked at me with those liquid pools of yumminess.

"What am I?" I teased, letting my soft fingers slide over his chest.

"You're everything. I missed you." His husky voice touched my soul in ways I never knew a man could. He reached his hand over the curve above my ass and gazed at me. I moistened my lips, looking at the grand specimen of hunk that laid in front of me. His head was propped up on one hand, the other moving across my stomach.

"I came to tell you about my brother. He's off you now. He's hunting down Jimmy and Blaze."

I watched the slight frown come over Diego's face as he pulled me closer to him. "I can't stop what the chapter is doing, but as long as we are good and in communication, we can stay one step ahead and prevent the war. Bloodshed is the last thing I want. I do want to get rid of those two slime buckets, though. They both need a good ass-kicking."

I wrapped my arms around him and sank into a blissful place.

"I agree..." I cooed.

He lifted my chin to look at me. "I love you so much. We aren't letting anything or anyone come between us, you hear me?"

"I hear you. I love you right back."

DIEGO

My beautiful Spanish princess was snuggled in my arms. I was her keeper. I bent my head, watching her stir silently as she slept. An epiphany hit me as I listened to her soft breathing. I wanted to marry Misty. I wanted to be with her in a very real way. I wanted to be the one she saw when she got back from studies in the evening. She stirred as her long lashes fluttered open. I stroked the outline of her face.

"Hey, papi."

"Hey," I said softly.

"What time is it? I gotta get to school! I've missed a couple of days."

I watched as her face turned to a frown.

"Why'd you miss school? I'm going to need a doctor soon."

She lightly tapped my face. "Don't say that. Nothing's going to happen to you. I just was worried and wanted to sort things out." She sat up and so did I.

"Want some coffee, toast before you go?"

"Yes. I have an idea. I know it's kind of out there but hear me out."

She swung her legs over the bed and slipped on her underwear. I put on a T-shirt from my closet and some track pants.

"Go ahead. I'm all ears." The light from the morning sun ran all through the lounge and kitchen area, causing me to adjust my eyes, rubbing them. She watched my movements as I turned on the water on the stove. "Baby, go ahead, tell me."

"Well, we know that Jimmy and Blaze are operating separately, right?" I dropped the toast in its slots with my back to her.

"You're telling me that. You're telling me that Palo ain't involved, so there's a high level of trust involved here. I say yes, plus the letters they're writing aren't that sharp."

"Okay, do you trust me or not? Look at me and say it," she demanded.

I turned to her with my hands leaning on the sink. My eyes pierced through hers. "Yes, I'm saying that I believe you. I do." I smiled at her.

"Your chapter and my brother's chapter are for the people of Merced, right?"

I pulled out plates and set them down in front of us. Her feline eyes in the morning made me want to pounce on her. Instead, I bent to her and landed a soft kiss on her swollen lips.

"Yes." I drew back. "I would say so. What are you thinking?"

"I'm thinking you both have the same cause. We all want to catch these suckers and get them off the streets. Why don't Las Balas and Outlaw Souls team up? You could patch up the bad blood between you both and forge alliances. Doesn't have to be like you're best buds, but if these guys are only two-deep, you should be able to take them."

I scoffed as the water boiled and I poured two cups of coffee for us. "Baby, you serious? I was thinking about it. But they have to have more people behind them because to make the threats they're making is career suicide and a death wish wrapped up together. You wanna know what I think?"

"Go, tell me. But you should think about what I just said." I handed her coffee over to her.

"They were trying to get us to start a war with Las Balas. I'm unconvinced that they want money. They put Las Balas at the bottom of the letter the first time, but we didn't direct the heat to Las Balas, so maybe they are trying to solely get the money now."

"I can't go to school like this. When is the drop?" Her hands shook as she drank her coffee.

"Baby, yes you can. I told you we're gonna handle this. Drop is tonight. I gotta talk to Ryder to see which way he's gonna swerve. I want him to go this route where I pretend to drop the money off so we can at least catch these suckers. That's the way I think it should go. We got a new sign-up who's in security." I sipped on my coffee as the toast popped.

"Okay, okay. Maybe I should have let my brother come see you. Both of you are reasonable men, maybe you would have sorted it out then and there," she mused.

"Maybe, maybe not. But we're here now. Go to school. I mean, what are you going to do? Sit around twiddling your thumbs? I'm keeping you outta this."

Her face blessed me with a small smile. "Okay. I'll do my best. Are your boys staying here 'til it's over?"

"Yes. They are."

She ate her toast in silence as I collected the two phones from my room and brought them to the front. By the time I got back, she was finished.

"Papi. I gotta go. Call me when you hear what's next. Please be safe. I love you." Her fiery Spanish eyes pleaded with me.

"I will. I'll be in touch." I kissed her with all of the fervor in me. I let her feel the depths of my love for her as I crushed her lips beneath me. I released her, breathless.

She packed up her bags and headed out to the car. I watched carefully as she got in and drove off. As soon as I saw the wheels in motion, I called Rick.

"Hello, Rick's Security Services. How can I help you?"

"Yo, Rick, it's Diego. I need your services."

"No problem. What are we talking about?"

"I'm dropping off a fake ransom amount tonight at Fahrens Park. I need your crew to be in place in case anything goes down. Can you work something out at short notice? What can you do?"

Rick didn't skip a beat. "Meet me at the warehouse in one hour."

I turned my phone and looked at the time: nine a.m. on the dot.

"Okay. Done."

"I got you. I'll bring gear and a few fellas. Ryder called me last night too. He gave me the four-one-one. I will be there and we'll set these bastards on fire."

"My man." The phone clicked dead. My stomach, as it had been the last few days, was rock hard from tension. I left the kitchen and jumped in the shower, letting the hot water wash away any thoughts of doubt. I felt almost certain we were going to war. As I dried off, I assessed the next steps. *Warehouse. Strap up. Strategy. Timing.*

I got dressed quickly. A faint beep I wasn't familiar with came from the kitchen bench. The cheap burner phone. A text message.

"Don't forget to come alone tonight. Times ticking bitch."

My impulses made me want to throw the phone against the wall. To hurl it out the fucking window. Sons of bitches. I strapped up, tucking my Smith and Wesson under my shirt. I grabbed my biker boots and put them on. I'd trimmed my beard up and tied back my hair, ready to get down to business. My phone rang, and Ryder's number came up.

"Hey, Diego. You ready? We meeting at the warehouse, right?"

"Yep. We are. Rick is in and bringing his guys. We're going to lay out the game plan."

"Okay. Done, see you there." Ryder clicked off. Death hung in the air like an old friend. But it wasn't about to be me or my crew that would perish. Jimmy Santos and Blaze Hernandez were about to become our bitches. I had everything I needed. I opened the door to my destiny. Determined, I mounted my bike and put my helmet on, ready to ride out. I arrived at the warehouse minutes later. As had been the routine of late, I double-checked all corners before rolling into the parking lot.

I noted a black truck with tinted windows was already parked. I saw a hand wave out the side of it. Rick. *Shit, he was lucky*. I was about to quick-draw on him.

"It's me. Chill."

"Okay." I was a few paces away from him. He was dressed in black with two other guys, tall, well-built and strong jawlines. Made for the fight. They both reminded me of army soldiers.

I held out my hand to Rick and was greeted with a firm handshake.

"Morning. You ready?" he asked.

"As I'll ever be. Who you got with you?" The two big boys were flanking both sides of Rick with their hands clasped in front of them.

He pointed to the left. "This here is Roberto, former kickboxer and army pro." He pointed to his left. "This here is

Alexander the Great, ex-army sergeant. We got the baddest in the game right here." I shook both their hands, but they were both silent. Jimmy and Blaze wouldn't stand a chance against either of these guys, let alone with Moves and Vlad in the mix.

"Damn straight. Let's go inside, fellas." I retrieved my keys from my pocket and punched in the alarm code. The dusty warehouse still held the two bikes I hadn't had a chance to look at since I was defending my motherfucking life. "Take a seat. Ryder and the boys will be here any minute, so no point repeating yourself." The familiar sound of the bike engines came in as soon as I mentioned Ryder. A formidable force: Yoda, Moves, Vlad, and Ryder. Four of the baddest dudes in the Outlaw club. My warehouse windows were still boarded up so I peeped out the front. Yep, all four on their two-wheeled machines. Ryder, leading the pack, came in and sat down with the three others. He gave them a hard once-over. He recognized Rick and leaned in to shake his hand. Vlad, Moves and Yoda followed. Everybody sat down.

"Hey, fellas. I'm Rick, for any of you that don't know me. I want to let you know you're in good hands. We got this. My two here are Roberto and Alexander the Great. Let's crush some heads." Rick flashed a criminal smile to the table. Ryder and Yoda nodded.

Moves and Vlad shook hands and grunted. *Must be enforcer code.*

"All right, look." Rick rolled out a map of Fahrens park. "Where are they asking you to drop off the money?"

I pointed to the spot on the map. "Right here."

"Okay, so if they have you make the drop here, we are going to wait in the shadows right here and here. Ryder, Vlad and Moves, I need you guys to stay rooted in these areas. I got a sniper gun, a silencer and a few other bad boys that will light them up nice, in case they don't come out 'til morning light to do the pick-up. We'll wait there and stake the joint out. They have to come pick it up. It's a popular park. My thinking is they will attempt to pick up a few hours later. They won't leave it. I know about these guys. They are dumb. Amateurs at this. But let's take it seriously. We don't know what they got going and who is backing them up. They can't be operating solo like this."

Ryder lit up and the smoke floated up in the air. "Doesn't make sense, them riding solo. You know what I mean? They mighty confident for a couple of thugs trying to start a pro' ring. Which is why I think they do have Las Balas behind them. They got a death wish otherwise."

"Could be their way of calling our bluff. We could be falling in a trap," I countered. My ears were thundering with my heartbeat.

Ryder sneered at me. "You gone soft up here in Merced, Diego. My directive is we send a warning flare to Las Balas. They're gonna know we got 'em by the balls. These fuckheads can't be solo."

I ignored his insult. "Could be they been planning and they have a crew together, already separated from Las Balas. Remember Jimmy Santos was in juvie a long time, prolly got a lot of friends in that time."

Ryder raised a brow at me. "You still seeing her, huh? You trying to protect your girl right now. I can see it in your eyes." I wanted to slap Ryder, but all eyes were on me.

"What about it? This ain't got nothing to do with Misty."

He gave me a wry smile.

"Uh-huh, now I know. Then you better let your girl know now, I'm sending a warning shot to Las Balas. We riding out, Diego. Handle it. Too late to back down now. Every one of you is strapped and locked. We following Rick's instructions. That's it." Ryder's finger hit the table in finality.

"Okay."

Ryder continued and butted out his cigarette. "This is a brotherhood. We are the Outlaw Souls and we need to defend our brothers and our territory. End of story. Ride or die."

Every one of us put our hands in the air and said in unison, "Ride or die!"

MISTY

The campus looked as vacant as I felt. The trees were swaying in the breeze and the perfectly manicured lawn with the usual college suspects was bare. I met Shauna and Celine in the cafeteria before class. Shauna had her usual bouncy glow and fresh lip gloss on.

"Hey, girl." She gave me the side-eye. "You've been looking kind of stressed out lately! What you got going on?"

"I have a lot going on. Life is crazy. Maybe I'm destined to be mixed up with bad boys for life."

She waved me off as we entered the glass doors of the cafeteria. Celine with her vibrant smile raced over to give me a hug.

"My God, I don't even know you anymore. You missed Biomed. I was crying without you!" Her enthusiasm made me laugh a little, easing the burden I felt.

"Hey, sit down and I'll grab the coffee. Celine, what do you want?" Shauna asked.

"I'll have a mocha," Celine replied, smiling brightly.

Okay. Misty, I already know what you want," Shauna said.

I saluted her and we found a spot away from the collective noise of everyone else.

"So, are you okay these days? "Celine asked, studying my face.

"Well, other than the fact the man I love might lose his life tonight and start a gang war with my brother, yeah, I'm okay."

Celine clapped her hand over her mouth, gasping. "That's ludicrous! Tell me everything. What the hell is going on?"

I sighed and twisted my hair. "Let's wait 'til Shauna gets back so I don't have to repeat myself."

"You sure you need to be mixed up with this guy?" Her nose wrinkled up, waiting for my reaction.

"I ain't got no choice. I'm in love with the guy. It's too late now. I gotta wait it out."

Shauna came back with three coffees on a tray. "Don't say nothing else, I wanna hear this. You haven't been to class all week, so I know this gotta be good."

"Diego's chapter might be starting a gang war with Las Balas. I can't get into why but if he does, I'm scared Diego might get caught in the crossfire. Remember those two guys at The Partition, Shauna?"

Shauna was locked in and listening hard. "Yep, those creepy toads at the bar. I remember. What about them?"

"Well, they are running game and are the ones responsible and now two rival gangs might go to war because of it. They were trying to start a pro' ring – like a pimp situation."

Shauna shook her head in disappointment. "Hunk of burning love ain't got nothing to with it, does he?"

"No. But I'm worried. I don't know how Palo is going to react. Funny thing is, both the clubs are trying to go straight."

Celine and Shauna sipped their coffees and I just stared at my cup. It was eleven-fifteen a.m. and I still hadn't heard from Diego. My stomach was turning over like it was churning butter.

"Why doesn't one of them just call the other and they sit down like men?"

I nodded my head up and down at Shauna. "Same thing I said. No need to go to war when they both want these guys off the streets. They are aiming their guns in the wrong direction."

My phone started buzzing. I immediately looked past my friends to the nearest exit. Shauna pointed to the back door. I mouthed "thank you" to her. Celine flashed me a pained look which annoyed me.

I stepped out into the cool breeze. "Talk to me, papi."

"Warn your brother. A shot is being fired to Las Balas. Let him know it has nothing to do with me. Tell him quickly." My throat constricted with fright. I coughed to open up my airways.

"Okay. Lemme get off the phone to call him. Shit. You okay?"

"Yep. I'm good. Don't go home if it's too hot. Please. Promise me. I don't know what's about to go down, but I know I love you. Hit me back once you call your bro'." My hands were about to fall off from shaking. Celine and Shauna were both watching me and frowning hard.

"Okay. I love you too. Please be careful and keep calling me with updates."

"No doubt. Hang in there, this will all be over soon."

I fumbled with my phone, nearly dropping it. I managed to not let it fall. I rang Palo and it went to voicemail.

Ayy, you've called Palo I'm not available right now but leave your name and number clearly and I'll hit you back.

DIEGO

The warehouse was a hive of activity. Guns were being locked and loaded. Click. Click. I squinted as I checked the ammo rounds in my Smith and Wesson. *Showtime*. Ryder had a silencer on the table, and he was twisting on the extension with a cigarette hanging out of his mouth. His dark eyes held no fear, only rock-hard resolve. Smoke hung over the table like the fog of death. Moves threw me a bulletproof vest. I put it on over the top of my black T-shirt. Vlad was already strapped and cracking his neck back and forth. Yoda had the garbage bag on the table with stacks of fake paper that he was concentrating on putting in. Stack by stack. Rick was testing out the walkie-talkies.

Testing, one, two, three, four... He handed one to Ryder to test. Rick walked to the other end of the warehouse. Ryder put down his silencer and spoke to him by pressing the side of the radio.

"Can you hear me?"

"Yup, loud and clear." Ryder's voice came through the other end of the radio.

Vlad found the on button for the radio and turned it on.

Bon Jovi streamed through the warehouse and Ryder and Yoda bobbed their heads to the beat. This was where the blood in my veins turned to ice. When I went to war, my mentality changed to numb out the situation I was facing.

"Listen up. Here's what's going to happen," Ryder said as he stroked his lion's beard. "I'm heading over to Merced now. Vlad and Moves are going to flank me. It's do or die."

I held my hand up. "Ryder, man, don't do this! You can't just roll up to their chapter talking crazy. I'm telling you. Misty told me the truth. Palo doesn't have nothing to do with this. You gotta trust me. She wouldn't put her brother in danger like that."

Ryder balked. "Fucking prove it!" He slammed his wiry hand flat on the table, making it shake.

Yoda, who had been silent most of the time, spoke up. "He's got a point, Ryder. Why don't you let me go in there? I'm more unassuming. Chill out. You can wait."

"If you think for one minute I'm just going to let you walk up in there unassisted, you're kidding yourself." Ryder eyeballed Yoda.

Yoda laughed at him. "Ah, Padre would be proud of you. Don't let your pride get in the way. If Palo isn't involved, he might be a useful ally. So let's put this to vote here among men. All those in favor of me walking in, put your hand up." Ryder glared at everyone in the warehouse, but all hands went flying up. Nobody wanted to die.

Ryder blew out cigarette smoke from his nose. "Okay, okay. Dammit."

"No time to waste. We need to know the truth. Let's ride out." Yoda signaled, and the chairs scraped as the crew got up from the table, ready for whatever. Ryder came over to me and stood close enough to my ear. "Your girl better be telling the truth."

"Ryder, back up from me. What I told you, I told you.

She's legit," I lashed out at him. I felt my fists bunch up involuntarily and my jaw lock into place.

"Ooooh, okay then. You really like this one. I see." Ryder smoothed his beard out and nodded. He looked me in the eye. "You better check where your loyalties lie."

He dropped his cigarette to the ground and stamped it out with his scruffy black biker boots. He spat to the side. Heat flashed through my body and Ryder's eyes dared me to act on the emotional impulse running through me. I moved past him out to the open. All the others were on their bikes, mounted and ready to ride out. Yoda signaled to follow him as the collective engine noise of the Outlaws revved, sounding like a small circus. We weaved in a single file right into the war zone. Misty's cat eyes flashed in my mind's eye. *I love you.* I let the Cali air singe my lungs. Today wasn't the day to die. We arrived, rolling eight deep, our engines idling outside the chapter house. A flag representing Las Balas swung in the wind. The chapter house was a small cry from our warehouse. A small, rinky-dink timber shed was more like it. Two beefy guys with full sleeves of tattoos and bald heads guarded the entry point. Both of them were packing heat. My stomach was tight. I wanted this shit to end. Yoda took his helmet off and looked at the boys.

"Stay right here. Don't move. Let me deal with them."

I flinched. Yoda was about to walk into the trap of death and I had the urge to run in with him. But instead, we waited.

Yoda got smaller and smaller as he approached the chapter house. Las Balas versus Outlaw Souls.

MISTY

I ran out of the cafeteria like the wind. I heard Celine and Shauna calling me, but I kept moving to my car. It felt like I was being drawn to Diego like a magnet. I had to get in touch with Palo. If I couldn't reach him by phone, I would go to the chapter house myself. I reached the car, my lungs burning from running so hard. My phone buzzed.

"Palo. Palo!" The urgency in my voice nearly stopped me from getting the words out.

"What the hell is going on? Talk to me!" He reacted from my voice.

"Outlaw Souls are coming. You need to tell them you have nothing to do with Jimmy and Blaze. There's a letter. Please." I struggled to get the words out of my mouth.

"Hold up. Wait. Wait. What the hell are you saying? Slow down and tell me what's going on!" Palo growled.

"Okay. Let me calm down." I sucked in a deep breath as I sat in the car. Tears were welling in my eyes as I spoke. A bad image of Diego being shot ran through my head. I stuffed it down. "Okay. There's a ransom on Diego's head. On the note, they used the name of Las Balas. Now Outlaw Souls think you're responsible. They are trying to extort money."

"So Jimmy and Blaze did this?" I could feel his anger through the phone screen.

"Yes. Outlaw Souls are coming to talk to you now. You need to do something. Don't start a war, Palo. I want you and Diego to live. He told me to tell you. They are coming now! Where the hell are you?" I said hysterically.

"I'm at the clubhouse. Everything's going to be all right. I got it covered. They're here already."

I banged the steering wheel. "Are you serious! Oh my God. Please. Palo, I'm praying for you. Please hold your fire! Please."

"Shhhh! I got it handled. Didn't I tell you that? Shut up. I gotta go. It's happening." The phone clicked dead and this was the most helpless I had ever felt in my life. I let the tears slide down my face as I put my hands together in prayer. I cranked the engine and let the tears drip. I rode off toward home. I would have to wait to hear. My phone was ringing. I glanced at it through the fog of my tears. Shauna. I couldn't talk to her right now. I breathed deep and knew somehow, someway, everything would work out as it should. I'd never wanted my family to be involved in Las Balas in the first place. Maybe Palo, if he made it out alive, would understand why. I arrived home a half-hour later. The tears had dried up, but not the hurt. I walked to the kitchen to grab a drink of water when my phone rang again. I wanted to throw the thing at the closest wall.

"Hey, baby."

"Diego!"

"We're good here."

"What the fuck do you mean 'we're good'?"

"I mean we met. You got the message to him, I see." I slid

down the wall in the kitchen, relief sinking me to the floor. I pulled my knees up to my chest and listened.

"Yes, I got it to him. What's the next bet?"

"Next bet is we teaming up. I'm coming in with the fake ransom, but we are rolling thirty-deep to take these thugs down. There will be no ransom given."

"Papi Chulo! You're not out of the woods yet. I mean, what if they shoot you? You don't know where Jimmy and Blaze will be. They could be anywhere."

"Shh. We got it now. Good news, you and I are out in the open now. Your bro' is cool peoples. I love you. You're a real one. You're my little gangsta'. A doctor, but you're a real one. Thanks for backing me. I love you. When I get out of this... it's going to be about you and me."

"I love you," I cooed. "I don't want anything happening to you."

"Hang in there, mamacita. Go to my place. In the potted plant on the left is a key. Right under the leaf. You gotta dig a little. I want you in my bed when I get home. Come stay with me. Start packing your shit. Come live with me. Think about it at least."

"Baby. I'll be there, just be careful and make it home to me tonight."

"Love you. Gotta go kick some ass. Bye."

DIEGO

Yoda stepped carefully to the clubhouse with his hands up. One of the beefy dudes stepped out in front of him. Ryder dismounted from the bike and moved toward him with his hands up as well. My nerves were tingling. Felt like walking into suicide if you asked me. A short bald-headed guy swung open the screen door to the chapter house and left it open. He gave the beefy dudes the head nod and they stepped back. To my surprise, the short guy raised his arm and waved to everyone to come in. He kept waving until we moved. Vlad, Moves and Rick looked at me and I looked at them. We idled our bikes into the space. The whole Outlaw crew was now on Las Balas turf, an unprecedented move in history.

We all dismounted from our bikes in succession and headed to the chapter house. Ryder stepped in first.

"Welcome. Let's have a friendly chat. It's all love here," the bald man said. Inside were the flags and the mottos of the chapter on the wall, like ours. Pictures hung in frames around the place, displaying the history of the club. Four big tables sat in the middle of the hall with chairs around them. "Hi, my name's Palo. I'm the new president here at Las Balas. As we all know, El Diablo is dead. We all know how he died, so let's cut to the chase, so we can defuse the tension here." His voice was clear-cut and professional. His face didn't resemble a killer. One tatt on the inside of his arm. I assumed it was the chapter branding. All the Outlaw boys took up space. Las Balas boys were at the other end of the table we sat at. Nasty-looking bunch, mostly of Spanish descent with dirty looks on their faces. Palo stood right in the middle of us. Vlad touched his back as he heard one of the dudes speaking in Spanish.

"Ayy, what did he say?" He nodded his head to Palo. Palo yelled something in Spanish to him and looked back to us.

"All right. So we got a problem with Jimmy Santos and Blaze Hernandez. Diego, where are you? Which one is dating my sister?"

I stood up and looked him dead in his face. He scanned me slowly.

"She really loves you. Don't fuck it up. So you're lucky enough to have a ransom on your head, huh?"

"Yeah, something like that," I mumbled. I couldn't quite work him out.

"So look, both of these clowns weren't taken care of as I asked. I got my man Rodriguez looking for them, but they must be hiding out. They used to live right around the corner. They are low-level crim's. But that doesn't mean they should be underestimated. I don't know who they roll with now, but I do know Jimmy has some heavies from his crim' days in his camp. I'm sure they will come with a crew. Let's team up and take care of them. Can we put our differences aside to do this, fellas?"

"We can do that. Having a chapter war was not on the agenda for Outlaw Souls either. We didn't come here looking for trouble," Ryder replied in a gruff voice.

"Okay. Then let's get it done. What plans you got? We will roll in with backup." Palo said.

From there, the conversation flowed with the next steps. Palo and Ryder mapped out the plan and arrangements. The whole experience was surreal, two rival gangs coming together to squash two scumbags. After two hours of deliberation and a step closer to the endpoint, we rode out.

The navy midnight sky had taken over from the cobalt-blue and the cool chill of Merced rushed past my face just like the adrenaline in my heart. Ten p.m and time for the show to begin. A phone call received earlier and a whole lot of heavy breathing confirmed things. I put them on speakerphone at the warehouse.

"You better be coming alone, otherwise there will be hell to pay."

"I'll be alone. Don't worry."

"Good, and make sure it's all there. We counting." The phone clicked dead before I could say anything else. Palo and his Las Balas crew were with us at the warehouse.

"That's him. I'd know the sound of Jimmy's voice anywhere."

Now we were thirty deep and I was the only one riding in. If I saw any sign of Jimmy or Blaze I was to hit the radio and cough. From there the party would start. By the time everyone locked in position, it was eleven p.m. I rode my bike into Fahrens Park and came to a stop in the parking lot. One lone light pole provided the light to the whole park. The same black pick-up that had been parked outside the warehouse was there. The trash can they'd told me to drop the money in was to my left. I had two garbage bags full of money. I shivered from the cold air, dropping the bags of fake money in the trash.

I pushed the radio button and coughed. Vlad and Moves

were coming on foot. Looked like there was only one vehicle in the park. That didn't mean there weren't more somewhere else. My eyes shifted and I stepped back from the trash can, ready to get back on my bike. An ugly shadow of a man stepped out of the black vehicle with the end of a pistol pointing at my face. He was about fifteen paces away. I felt the rage bubble up. I knew if I pulled for my gun, the guy would shoot out of fear. I put my hands up instead.

"So you're the guy, huh? Stay right there. Didn't expect to see us, huh? Thought we would pick it up in the morning, right?" I still had my hand on the radio button so the other guys could hear it. Now the other side of the car door opened and the fat guy got out, cracking his knuckles.

"I don't want any trouble, guys. I dropped off the money, so that's it."

I saw the outline of his square jaw. "Oh, you think that's it, huh? No, no. That's not how this works. You're getting in the car with us. We got some treats for you. You're going to come in useful for us."

I watched the weasel go to the trash can. He picked the bags out and headed back to the truck with them. I sat on my bike quietly, not moving. I kept my eyes on the trash but behind the tree in front of the trash can was Vlad. Couldn't miss his shadow. I didn't want to draw attention to him so I sat still and watched the weasel's eyes in the moonlight.

The other one spoke. "You can either come easily or we can make this a situation for you."

"You're going to wish you didn't do this. You might not live to regret it," I said with an eerie quietness.

"What the fuck you say?" the weasel – Blaze – said as he raised his gun. Vlad, in one large stride, grabbed him around the neck and put him in a sleeper hold. He turned his neck and snapped it. The fat guy, scared out of his wits, started moving back to the vehicle and pointed his gun, ready to shoot, but he fumbled. By the time he did, Rick had a gun at the back of his head.

Vlad signaled to me. "Go now, Diego. Your job is done, we got it from here. Go. *Move*." I mounted my bike and left the scene. All the guys were waiting on standby.

"Let's roll," I said. The mighty roar of the engines picked up as everyone rode out their respective ways. That was how it worked. No questions, no information disclosed. Once the enforcers took over you got the hell out of the way. You never spoke of the incident again. *That's biker code. It doesn't happen in case of police interrogation. Bikers don't do snitching.* We all split at various points on the highway, Ryder saluting me as he headed home on the freeway.

I was headed home to my girl. After all the hype, it turned out to be an anticlimactic ending and a quick clean-up for Outlaw Souls.

MISTY

I found the key just like he said. I had to get my nails dirty a little but I didn't care. I fitted the key in the lock, slotting in perfectly. I walked into Diego's apartment. The heating was on and helped me thaw out from the chilly night air. I slid my hands across the table, remembering our first date. The candlelit dinner. The way our lips came together so seamlessly as if they belonged. I walked around to the sink, the place where Diego had stood barefoot with his low-slung jeans. Every time he was in the kitchen, I wanted him to take me on the countertop. I loved watching the way he moved so gracefully around the kitchen.

A bottle of red wine was tucked away near the stove. I needed something to calm my overwhelmed senses. I opened the cabinet, got out a glass, and let the chug of the red wine splash into it. I closed my eyes and begged for the tension in my shoulders to subside. I sipped the red and let it hit my system, mellowing me out a little. I looked at my phone. Twelve p.m. and he still wasn't here. I put the glass down on the kitchen bench as a vision flashed in my mind of Diego dead with a bullet in his chest. I closed my eyes again and took another sip. I found my eyes drooping after a few minutes; all the energy expended from worrying and running around had taken its toll. I brought my things into Diego's room. I slipped into his shower and let the hot water kiss my skin and warm me up. The buzz from the red had worn off and I was sleepy. I slipped under the covers naked while I waited for Diego. My eyes drifted in and out. I wanted to keep them open but they wouldn't comply. The next thing I felt was a warm hand reach to cup my breast and knead my nipple. I felt the size of the palm and the ridges on the inside of his hand. I knew for certain it was Diego.

"Diego!" I turned in the dark to feel for his chest and he wrapped me up, bringing me into him.

"Baby. We made it. I'm here." He sounded relieved. He roamed all over my face with light kisses and I giggled.

"I'm so happy you're here. Are you okay? Are you hurt?" I saw the smile in the darkness as I stroked his chin.

"Relax. Everything is okay. It's all been done. Those bitches will never bother you or me ever again. I'm just glad you're in my bed. Mmm." Diego nuzzled his head into the crevice of my neck and I stroked his hair.

I'm so glad you're alive. I love you, papi chulo!"

"I love you too, mamacita. It's been a long ride. Let's go to sleep."

"Okay." I turned around and he spooned me from the back. I had the most peaceful sleep that I'd had in months. I woke up to the morning sun and the soft hum of the radio. I stretched backward and felt for Diego, but no one was there. I sat up with my hair flowing in every direction. Finally, the madness was over. Diego entered minutes later with a hot coffee and those low-slung jeans I liked. In his other hand was a plate of toast. *It's the little things like this that make me love him more.*

"Good morning, beautiful." He kissed my lips with such tenderness I thought I might cry. I took the coffee in my hands, watching the steam rise up and the rich aroma fill my nostrils.

"Good morning," I croaked. "I definitely have to go in to school today. I've missed classes."

"Did you miss classes because of me?"

"Yes. Well, because of the situations going on."

He kissed the side of my forehead as he walked out and came back with his coffee. "I don't want you to miss out on anything else. I want to ask you something as well..." I peeked over my coffee, amused at his uncertainty. "Would you move in here with me?"

I paused for a little deliberation as my lips curved into a smile. "Yes, I would."

"You're making me a happy man right now. I adore you."

"Funny how things work out."

"Sure is." The phone buzzed from the kitchen, and Diego jumped up. For some reason, he had it on speaker.

"Hey, Ryder."

"Hey, Diego," a deep voice said.

"You did good. Keep rolling with your chapter. You stood for what was right and didn't back down. You're a real Outlaw. I'm proud of you, now more than ever. I'm glad Yoda backed you to open Merced."

Diego smiled hard. "That means a lot coming from you, OG."

The man with the deep voice laughed. "Your girl must be a good one for you to go out on a limb like that. We might still be opposing forces, but Las Balas got a couple of stand-up people in there."

"For real. She's a keeper, for sure." Diego rubbed my knee, winking at me as I ate my toast. "At least we know we got some allies up here."

"Absolutely. I'm sorry I doubted you in the first place."

"Yeah. It got a little rough between us, but I understand your point of view."

"It's all good. We are a family. Sometimes we fight and then we make up."

"Look, I'll let you go, I'll check in with you later in the week."

"All right, bye, Diego. Thanks."

"Bye."

I rubbed Diego's back and gave him a naughty smile.

"I'm a keeper?"

"Yep, you're a keeper." He took the mug from my hand and set it on the bedside table.

I waggled my finger at him. "Don't start that. I won't make it to school again."

He laughed. "I guess I can wait. You will be waking up with me from now on so it's all good."

After some more morning time snuggling, I got up and dressed.

For the first time in weeks, I arrived on time. I texted Shauna to meet before class. I was back to floating on campus.

Shauna, with her usual bright colors and sunny disposition, studied my dreamy face and hugged me tight.

"I was so worried about you! My God, girl, what went down with you?"

"Oh, the usual, ransom notes, bikers and rival gangs coming together to fight scumbags," I said flippantly.

Shauna doubled over in laughter, putting her hands on her knees. Her eyes leaked with hysterical tears as she tried to take in what I'd said. I just stood there with a wry smirk on my face.

She watched my face. "Holy shit, you're not kidding!" She

grabbed my jacket as we ordered our coffees and walked to class. "Oh my God, tell me everything…"

Harmony in my world had been restored. Turns out the bad boy was for me. I just needed the right one. A Spanish papi with a heart of gold. One thing is for sure; Diego and I were destined for a wild ride, and I would be right by his side.

EPILOGUE

Two years on in Merced, California, and things looked a lot different. First off. I graduated from seven long years of college, achieving my dream of becoming a doctor. I'd wanted to be a cardiologist, or so I thought, but I was content for now to start my residency. That was enough. Besides, I had new dreams with my husband-to-be. I remember the day I graduated. I threw my royal navy blue cap high up in the air.

"I'm so proud of you. You're about to be out here saving lives and making the world a better place," Diego whispered in my ear as I stepped down from the makeshift podium. I scanned the oval as I looked around at my loved ones and all the others that were graduating with me. My brother, my cousins, my mother, my father, my classmates. All of these people had invested in my future.

Shauna and I danced on the lawn like goofballs. "We made it! We made it! We're gonna be doctors." I hugged her tight. Without her, I might not have made it through. Shauna ended up working at the University of California Medical Center in San Francisco. We spoke most days, comparing case notes and seeing one another at conferences. She ended up dating one of the doctors from her hospital and was now happily in a relationship. The apartment ended up being too small for me and Diego. We moved to a bigger place. A house in the Merced 'burbs with a garden as we settled into a nice rhythm of coupled-up life.

One day, eighteen months into our relationship, I came home dog tired from rounds in the emergency room at the local Merced hospital. Diego was catering to me as always, and I had my feet up on the couch.

"You've had a long day, mamacita."

I looked at him wearily. "Yes I have."

He kneaded the knots of my feet with his hands. Felt good. I had my eyes closed, enjoying the moment with a glass of wine on the table. "Would you consider spending all of your long days with me like this?"

I opened one eye and looked at him. "Of course, why wouldn't I?"

He grinned. My hours had been so long at the hospital in addition to the rise of Diego's chapter, it felt like we were drifting.

"We've both been so busy, but I want to say to you, I want to spend forever and a day with you. I want to make a lifetime of memories. I want to fight and make up with you and ride through everything together. I want to be old and gray and live to tell the tales of our extraordinary things we've done together. Misty Narvaez, will you marry me?" My eyes flew open as right there on the couch on an ordinary Wednesday night as my Spanish lover, best friend and badass biker proposed to me. I leaped up and into his arms.

"No question. I love you, papi. Let's get married."

"Wait. I have something for you." Tucked in his low-slung jeans was a beautiful white diamond with a cluster of smaller diamonds around it.

I kissed him a thousand times." When did you? How did you?" Shock was all my face could show.

"When you were at work, of course." He slid the rock onto my finger, completing our union of love.

Life between us just got better after that. It became known in Merced, especially in the biker community, that we were the bridge between the divide of rival gangs. In fact, Outlaw Souls and Las Balas became known for their charity and community service partnership for wayward youth. Both of them donated to Doctors Without Borders and even made the national paper for their unified front. I would never forget the day.

"Baby, I'm so proud of you. Thirty men in your chapter and the business is taking off. The sky's the limit for you," I gushed, looking deep into his eyes.

"I learned that from you. You make me a better man. I couldn't stand beside someone like you and be a bum. You wouldn't have it."

I giggled. "You're right, I wouldn't! You did good, baby. Real good."

Ryder accepted us. Palo accepted Diego and the respect level between them was high.

"Take care of my sister and we'll always be good. You have my respect since Jimmy and Blaze." I smiled as I remembered the day when Palo let his guard down. Meant a lot to me.

"I will. She's my heart, you'll never need to worry. Between the both of us, we'll make sure she's good." The Spanish way of two men standing on either side of me.

So here we were, two years in, planning a wedding, sitting on our back porch.

"I want a cupcake cake. What do you think, babe?"

"Whatever you want, as long as I get the chocolate fondue foundation."

"That's a lot of sweets, Diego."

"Well, we have big Spanish families. You know both of ours love their sweets. That's how it is."

"Cupcakes it is."

"Who are you gonna ask to be your maid of honor?"

"Shauna. Who's your best man?"

"Prolly Yoda. We go way back. He took me under his wing in the early days of the chapter."

"I know you have a lot of stories."

Diego looked at me softly as the Merced sun's burnt-orange face faded behind the California hills.

"I sure do, and you and I have plenty more to tell our children in the future. Speaking of babies, should we get busy making one?" Diego smiled.

I giggled at Diego's boldness, something I always loved. "And may they have your fearlessness and that full lion's mane of hair." I ran my fingers through his thick dirty blonde hair and he responded by scooping me up in his strong manly arms, lifting me to the threshold.

One thing that's for sure is I was willing to ride and die for mine. *Will you for yours?*

———

Read on for a sneak peek of **OUTLAW SOULS BOOK 6** featuring Colt, who is doing time for a crime he unwittingly committed for the Outlaw Souls when he meets social worker Amber. She is assigned to his daughter, Bella, after her mother dies. Sparks fly immediately, but when Amber needs his help to save her brother's life, he steps up. With countless obstacles to overcome, will they ever get the chance at a fresh start and at love? **Buy now!**
FREE with Kindle Unlimited.

———

Thank you so much for reading this book. If you liked **BLADE, please leave a review for it now.**

Join My Newsletter
Click here to sign up for my newsletter for deals, sneak peeks, and more.

SNEAK PEEK! COLT (OUTLAW SOULS BOOK 6) PROLOGUE

Four and a Half Years Ago

"You have the parts?"

"Yeah, I do. When can I pick them up?"

"You got 'till noon tomorrow. They'll be available at the usual meeting spot. Bring the truck around back, and make sure you're alone. You have half an hour to load up."

I responded with a slow head nod. I understood the steps. I'd been following them for months without a hiccup. "Done. See you then."

The Merced sun was showing no mercy, beating down on the back of my neck. At the ripe old age of thirty-five, my bones ached as if they were attached to a fifty-year-old. I should have been used to the burning heat. After all, I grew up as a California farm boy, and I still lived on the farm.

I would sit by the brook some days as a teenager and watch the rocks skim over the water. That was when I wasn't getting on and falling off of horses.

A man I'd looked up to all my life—Clive Winters, my father—would tell me every time I fell off, "You are not going to let that horse get the best of you, now are you? I didn't raise a softie. Come now, son. Get back on the horse."

SNEAK PEEK! COLT (OUTLAW SOULS BOOK 6) PROLOGUE

I smiled wryly. I used to think he was surely out to get me, to see me fail. Now I knew something entirely different.

I wouldn't give up my country lifestyle for anyone. I remembered how the red, tawny dirt swirled in the air while I straddled the paddock fences, rebuilding them from years of wear and tear. All that work on the farm gave me the strength of a lion. That strength was distributed on my six-foot-one frame nicely. My hair was pretty shaggy and bleached blond from the Cali sun. I remembered the distant calls of wild coyotes in the cool of the night.

On my farm, we ran with ten chickens, and all of them laid. One old rooster, affectionately known as Croak, was the alarm for first light and dusk. The horses on the farm were my pride and joy. I spent the most time with them. I had three purebred caramel Palominos and one sleek black mare.

We grew all sorts of products on the farm, too—carrots, onions, strawberries, and green beans. I'd taken over the farm from my tired and weary parents in my late twenties. My parents were in their sixties, and they both wanted a break.

"We want you to run the farm, son. Carry on the Winters name. Think you can do that for us?" my father asked me one day.

"Yep. I got you, Pop," I'd said. "I wouldn't have it any other way."

I knew the farm and the lay of the land like the back of my hand, and I had since I was a kid. That became that. We got the papers signed so that the farm was in my name, and I kept successfully running it. I managed to run the place with a firm but fair hand and a tight-knit crew who were loyal to the Winters. When the end of the crop season finished, they all received nice bonuses to take home to their families.

My other love, motorcycles, gave me the same freedom my horses did, which is why I had a custom chopper with a stallion drawn on the chrome. The moonlight sat behind the horse, which was rearing, its front legs in the air. When my bike developed some problems, I took her into the Merced motorcycle repair shop. That's how I first linked up with the Outlaw crew. They were a really cool crew. So I joined and didn't think too much about it. I got my vest a while later, thinking it was just a crew I would ride with every now and then. As time wore on, the business was revealed to me.

"Hey, we got a job for you if you're interested." Vlad, the Outlaw Souls enforcer, stood solid, tall, and deadly in the warehouse quarters I worked at. It was a chop shop with really good prices for customers. Again, I didn't think anything of it, and I didn't ask any questions. I probably should have.

"Sweet. What's the job?" The farm was kind of slow at that time of year since we were between crop seasons.

"I need you to collect some auto parts and ship them down to La Playa. Ortega Autos are going to utilize them." When Vlad spoke, you listened. He represented death. His eyes penetrated your soul, and his dark aura let you know what time it was. He wasn't the guy you wanted to fuck with.

"Say no more. Where are the pickups running from?"

"They're running out of an old warehouse in Merced. I'll give you the address. All you have to do is the stock inventory and organize the shipments. I've already set up the deal with my Russian counterparts."

"Okay. Sounds like a sure bet."

He pressed his large hand on my shoulder.

"It is a sure bet. Just don't fuck it up. These guys are executioners by trade, and they don't give two fucks about shooting you in the head. You'll get a monthly kickback. Should help you with the farm expenses." Vlad winked.

"Sure would be nice. I could use the help right now. Things are a little tight between seasons. Plus, I have Bella's kindergarten fees coming up. Anna is working a little, but not much."

Vlad winked again and readjusted his leather jacket. "Thought as much, which is why I offered you the job."

Anna was my Bella's mother and a real fiery brunette rebel from the streets. Despite her flaws and for all her bravado, I could always see through to the heart of her, and that thing was golden, just like the California hills. I'd taken her off the streets. She was a meth cook, and since Bella had been born, she seemed to have settled into her purpose in life. On that day, like any other in Merced, I kissed her goodbye in the morning.

"Bye, baby. Have a great day," she said, and I bent my head to her lips. "Bella, say bye to Daddy. He has to go to work now."

The innocence of my baby girl softened every part of my heart as I held her in my arms. Her sandy brown hair was in pigtails. Her big brown eyes were the same color as her mother's, but she had my tight cheekbones. Her tiny lips reached the side of my cheek for a peck.

"Okay. Daddy has to go earn the bacon. See you and Mommy tonight." I grinned at her.

"Okay, Daddy. I love you. You can put me down now."

She wriggled free of my arms, and I laughed. There was never a dull day with four-year-old Bella.

The dirt scuffed my tan leather cowboy boots as I kissed my horses goodbye in the stables, a morning ritual I'd carried with me since my days on the farm with my father.

Today was the standard pick-up day. Nothing shaking. A normal day like any other. I straddled and mounted my bike, heading into the Merced warehouse. When I pulled up, the radio was blaring, and the warehouse door was open.

Diego greeted me with a smile. "Hey, brother. How you doing?"

"Doing great. About to head out to this pick-up. We are moving these parts hard. Must be a lot of repairs coming out of La Playa."

Diego, with his dirty blond hair, blew out a breath. Diego was the maestro of bikes. He could bring any bike back to life. He'd built the chapter from the ground up, and now it was forty members deep. He stood another inch taller than me, and if you didn't know us well, you would say we were brothers. Diego's Argentinian heritage made him a shade darker than me, though.

"You're telling me. There is a ludicrous amount of parts being used. They need more people in the chop shop. It's so busy. They ain't got the room. I run my motorcycle repair shop, though, so I don't want to be involved with the parts."

"For real? Guess it's cheap for La Playa. We are getting them at a heavily discounted rate. As far as being involved goes, sometimes you just have to do what you have to do." I sneered.

"You got that right."

"Okay, I'm going to go ahead and ride out. The truck here yet?"

Diego wiped down one of the bikes he was working on, stepping back to assess it.

"Yup. It's out back. Here are the keys. Be careful. The only reason I'm giving them to you is that Vlad isn't here." He reached in his pocket and threw the keys at me.

With one hand, I caught them.

"See you when you get back."

I strolled to the small truck and cranked the engine. On the way over, my stomach turned. A pressure sat in the cavern of my lungs as the green and gold California hills rolled by. As I approached the gate, my breathing became labored. I pulled into the warehouse and reversed in for easy access. I had the key to the roller door, but for some reason, it was already open. That sinking feeling came back. Maybe they'd left it open, ready for me. I sat in the truck for a minute, shaking off the paranoia.

Languidly, I let my cowboy boots hang out the side and stepped out of the truck. I came around the back and opened the latches. The warehouse was cold and dark. Again, nothing to worry about. A standard at this stage. Only two Russians met me, and they stood in the dark with long leather jackets and gloves on. Only the long strip of light from the outside door made them visible.

"Good. You're on time," I quipped.

"We got those parts you need."

"Perfect, I'll get them right now." I started toward the back of the truck. In the shadows, I witnessed their horror-stricken faces along with mass confusion.

"What's the problem?" I asked them.

I missed the light footsteps behind me, but I didn't miss the barrel of the pistol to the side of my temple. I balled my hands into fists, ready to knock this motherfucker out.

Then the words of the law rang through my ears. "Freeze! You're under arrest. Put your hands in the fucking air, now!"

Several navy blues raided the place like worker ants, snatching the duffel bag from my fingers. The two Russians looked at me closely. One of them mouthed, "Don't snitch," and ran a line across the bottom of his chin.

I put my hands behind my head, and all I saw was Bella and her cute toothy smile flashing through my brain. Anna and her raven hair. I didn't know if she would cope if I went in. I couldn't hear their muffled voices as they read me my rights. They faded away at that point. The sirens and the lights surrounded me as I said nothing. On that day, my luck ran out, and so did my time.

SNEAK PEEK! COLT (OUTLAW SOULS BOOK 6) CHAPTER ONE

Four and a half years later...

"*Let's go, cell block six! You got half an hour in the yard! Let's go. Let's go!*" A burly prison guard's voice perforated D block as the warning came before the cell doors clicked open. I licked my chapped lips and stepped out of my cell cautiously. I bent my head down and stepped straight into line, that was the drill. I did a head count, about thirty other guys were being let out to the yard or the common area as well. One small window of freedom is all we got every day at USP Atwater. I welcomed the time. My spot in the jail was cemented, nobody would touch me. When I first came in six years ago I had to prove my spot, real quick.

The sneers came through the cell bars. "Look at this, Roger. We got ourselves a new little bitch to play with." A roughneck who was known for making new inmates his play-toys got the word of me. I looked that motherfucker in the eyes as I passed his cell.

"Lissssen up you piece of shit. I'll kill your mother, your father, your brothers, your cousin and anyone else that tries it in here. You hear me?" I let him feel the cold chill of my eyes on his face, while I held the fury of twenty men in my balled up fists. He took a beat to size me up.

"Tough guy huh? You talk like that off rip you must know something." He replied, lifting his chin at me. He was a huge guy with shoulders like small boulders merged into his neck. He gave me a gruesome smile with his big dirty eyes. From the looks he wasn't in the Penn for armed robbery. He had a quote tattooed across his neck and multiple face tattoos. I knew his type. Plus, he was too big to take me down. But hey, prison law versus street law is different.

"You got that right. I'm an Outlaw, 'til the day I die." I yelled loudly as I passed the guy's cell. The weedy guard who brought me in was silent the whole time. He opened my rusty cell door where one other guy laid on a bolted bunk bed. In the corner was a single basin, the tap dripped continuously and the toilet smelt well - like shit. One single TV on a swivel was up high in the corner. The faint lime green paint was peeling off the walls and a few books were stacked on two simple shelves.

"Welcome to your new home, for the next six years." The prison guard sneered as he pushed me in the back into the hellhole. So to get out of the cell was our version of heaven.

I moved around a small grassed area with four walls. It was big enough to fit about fifty men. First thing I did was stretch out my neck and look at the open blue sky. A weight bench had two guys getting in their reps.

"C'mon Marty. We got three to go. Max rep sets." Grunts came from a guy underneath the weights as he strained to lift. I watched as the veins pulsed against the side of his neck, threatening to burst. Eventually, he heaved the barbell off his chest.

One other guy was skipping in a nice rhythm, dripping sweat on the grimy pavement. A stiff looking correctional officer stood in the corner watching us all like hawks. He had a baton firmly slotted in his holster and a taser on the other side. His mouth was opening and closing with the gum he was popping. The guards name was Chester and he was a complete sucker. If I got my farm hands on him on the outside I would have snapped his neck in half like we snapped our chickens necks back in the day. Chester put me in the hole for three days when I got in a scrap. Shit wasn't my fault guy tried to pull a fucking razor out on me. That's before I knew the prison hierarchy game. I flashed back to the memory, not a time I would forget easy,

"You talking back, boy?" Chester hissed in my ear. He had me in a strong chokehold as he yanked me off Lopez. My air supply was tied up as I grabbed his forearm to release it for breath. Lopez being the bitch he was tried to blame me for his drug shipment being smuggled in the wrong cell. I was well matched physically to take Lopez. He was about 6'1 like me, heavily muscled and quick with his speech and his movements. He ran with a drug crew on the streets called the Merced Mercenaries. A teardrop sat right under his left eye. His caramel complexion and honey coloured eyes made him a target for those who wished he dropped the soap in the showers. He didn't worry about that as he was the drug insider and supplied over half the jail.

"Heard you knew about the shipment and you moved it player." The right side of Lopez's mouth turned up as he spoke to me. He'd just walked into the door with his fist in his other hand. The washing machines whirred around us as I finished my laundry. No other people were in the laundry room. I picked up one of the white sheets from the dirty laundry basket and wrapped it around my hand. My back tensed up as Chester circled. I let my peripheral vision govern his footwork.

"Oh yeah? Where you hear that from? Because I don't

have anything to do with your little operation." I replied slowly.

"I know you're not about to do nothing wit' that sheet. I fucking know you're not." Lopez closed the laundry door behind him and moved a step towards me. I bent my knees and hunched in position. I searched his body for weapons. He spat out a razor from the side of his mouth. He held up the gleaming piece of metal and grinned.

"See this? This here is what I got for boys like you." He looked away briefly, but lunged at the same time, trying to catch me unawares. I retracted my head back as the breeze from his swing tried to connect with my face. I let out a whooshing sound. I circled with him and we started to dance.

"Snow told me you slashed his face. So you think you gonna do that to me?" My hands hung low on both sides and stretched my fingers out ready to pop him in the jaw. I looked at his body and it was wide open.

"That's right bitch. Now it's your turn." Lopez lunged as I saw the metal pass the right side of my face. I bumped into the side of the washing machine and the edge jabbed me in the side. I held it for a quick minute.

Lopez grinned as his eyes narrowed he swiped again and this time I tunneled my left fist into his lower intestine. He coughed as the impact made him draw up into himself.

"How you like that? Huh? I fucking told you I ain't got nothing to do with your drugs."

He yelped. "You bastard." He staggered and I thought that would be the last of it. He put his foot out near my left leg and my foot came out from under me. I fell on one knee to the ground, I tried to stabilize with one hand. I wasn't quick enough; he ran the razor across the edge of my neck. My super lightning reflexes made it so it was just a nick but I felt the blood trickle down my throat. The red shadow

SNEAK PEEK! COLT (OUTLAW SOULS BOOK 6) CHAPTER ONE

pounding behind my eyes sent me into overdrive and burrowed my head into his stomach, blasting him into the back of the washing machine on the other side of the room.

I felt the air run out of his lungs as he slumped to the ground and the razor fell to the concrete slab. The siren went off and my eyes flew to the camera in the corner. I quickly approached the door to leave but on the other side was Chester. He put his hand out.

"Stop right there! What the fuck is going on!" He took one look at Lopez slumped in the corner and one at me.

"I was defending myself! I swear-" He came straight for me and laced me in a chokehold.

"You're going to simmer down in solitary confinement, Outlaw. This is my prison and we don't let shit like that fly." That was my first year introduction. I would never forget it.

Back to now...One stationary camera in the back left hand side focused on the yard's activity. Not all thirty men came to the yard. Some others went to the common area. A dilapidated room the size of two living rooms. Not enough for 1000 inmates to congregate. That's too much testosterone for one area. I wanted to get some sets in and talk to some of the old timers in the yard.

I strolled over to Austin who was holding the barbell for another guy. Austin was in his sixties but strong as an ox. His eyes and ears were to the ground in the prison and he knew everything. I placed the barbell back in its lot as the guy lifted his head off the bench.

Austin with his scrappy grey beard and bald head smiled a toothy grin as I came towards him.

"Hey young buck. How you holding up?" He raised his brow at me as he adjusted his gloves.

I pointed at him. "Stay right there. I wanna talk to you 'bout something. I need a spot too."

Austin nodded and waited til I got under the bar. "Right.

You wanna know how you can get a message to Frank right?" He leaned over the bar and turned back to the guard.

"Damn straight." I flattened my back against the bench with my feet firmly on the ground.

"Ok. What's the message young buck?" Austin knew my weights and slid the heavy steel plates on either end of the bar.

"No message. I need a face to face. That's my Outlaw brother. I know he's coming out of the hole from last month. That place will send you to your grave early."

Austin's grave laugh rang out. "You got that right. Solitary is the place for no-one. Many have hung themselves down there. But you learned. Stay away from Lopez. His sole mission is to send inmates to solitary. If he views you as a threat he starts trouble deliberately. The guards are in on it too. That's why Chester knew when to come in like he did. You're not special. It's their one- two combination. I'm glad that sorry son of a bitch got transferred." I shook my head as I felt the weight bear down on me when Austin handed me the weight. I took it as my arms shook at with the new test.

"That's it. Hold it. You got it. Lower down slow. Let's go. I'm testing you today." I sucked in and exhaled on the push up. At 75% Austin took the weight. He threw me the towel to wipe my face.

"So you ain't snitch huh?"

"Nope. That's not how we do it in the Outlaws. Got me five years. But I just gotta keep my nose clean for the next six months you know. "

"Could have been no years. Vlad made that a situation for you. Frank told me."

"I know, but now he owes me. No better situation than to be in the driver's seat."

"That's on account of you making it out of her alive. Now let me tell you something. These jerks can smell when you're

SNEAK PEEK! COLT (OUTLAW SOULS BOOK 6) CHAPTER ONE

about to get close to being let out. They're going to test you. Make it hard. Try to corner you and get more stacked on your sentence. I wouldn't be coming out to the yard no more if I were you."

Austin lifted the weight down on my chest again as I set up for the second set. He lowered as my arms burned from the lactate buildup. I inhaled on the drop and exhaled straining hard on the lift. Austin put his fingertips under put and didn't lift the burden. I thought the weight would drop on my chest.

"C'mon now. Quit being pussy. You got it in you. C'mon." I grunted with the last drop of force I had lifting the bar an inch higher. Austin assisted from there.

"There you go. We'll make one out of you yet." The adrenaline from lifting kept me sane in this hellhole.

"I hear you about staying low key. I just have this one thing I gotta get done before I leave here and I know Frank can help me."

"No doubt he can. I'll set it up and send word to you." Austin watched the guard as he made the rounds around the perimeter of the yard.

"I don't know how you've made it all these years in here Austin." Austin with his wispy white hair laughed.

"I've weathered bitter storms my boy, but none greater than losing my wife in the summer of '89. I didn't care to live after that anyway."

"You shot the perp nine times. That's crazy." I replied.

Austin whistled through his teeth. "Yup that's what happens when armed robbery goes wrong. I don't regret it though. Not one shot. That guy tried to come for my baby. I had to defend her. I didn't know the guy would keep a gun in the house."

Austin received life in prison for the murder and armed robbery. He knew most of the lifers in the pen.

"Put me in touch with Frank. I want to talk to him."
Austin with his humble and wise eyes nodded. "Ok."

I can't wait for you to find out what happens with Colt and Amber...

Purchase COLT (OUTLAW SOULS BOOK 6) FREE with Kindle Unlimited.

ALSO BY HOPE STONE

All of my books are currently available to read FREE in Kindle Unlimited. Click the series link or any of the titles to check them out!

Guardians Of Mayhem MC Series

Book 1 - Finn

Book 2 - Havoc

Book 3 - Axle

Book 4 - Rush

Book 5 - Red

Book 6 - Shadow

Book 7 - Shaggy

LEAVE A REVIEW

Like this book?
Tap here to leave a review now!

Join Hope's newsletter to stay updated with new releases, get access to exclusive bonus content and much more!

Join Hope's newsletter here.

Tap here to see all of Hope's books.

Join all the fun in Hope Stone's Readers Group on Facebook.

ABOUT THE AUTHOR

Hope Stone is an Amazon #1 bestselling author who loves writing steamy action packed, emotion-filled stories with twists and turns that keep readers guessing. Hope's books revolve around possessive alpha men who love protecting their sexy and sassy heroines.

Learn more about all my books here.

Sign up to receive my newsletter. You'll get free books (starting with my two-book MC romance starter library), exclusive bonus content and news of my releases and sales.

If you liked this book, I'd be so grateful if you took a few minutes to leave a review now! Authors (including myself) really appreciate this, and it helps draw more readers to books they might like. Thanks!

DIEGO: AN MC ROMANCE
Book Five in the Outlaw Souls MC series
By Hope Stone

© Copyright 2020 - All rights reserved.

It is not legal to reproduce, duplicate, or transmit any part of this document in either electronic means or in printed format. Recording of this publication is strictly prohibited and any storage of this document is not allowed unless with written permission from the publisher except for the use of brief quotations in a book review.

This book is a work of fiction. Any resemblance to persons, living or dead, or places, events or locations is purely coincidental.

f

Printed in Great Britain
by Amazon